SNOW AT THE DOME

by

Estherlouise McDonough MSW, LCSW

With contributions from Patrick D. McDonough

DORRANCE PUBLISHING CO
EST. 1920
PITTSBURGH, PENNSYLVANIA 15238

The contents of this work, including, but not limited to, the accuracy of events, people, and places depicted; opinions expressed; permission to use previously published materials included; and any advice given or actions advocated are solely the responsibility of the author, who assumes all liability for said work and indemnifies the publisher against any claims stemming from publication of the work.

All Rights Reserved
Copyright © 2019 by Estherlouise McDonough MSW, LCSW

Photos courtesy of Patrick D. McDonough

No part of this book may be reproduced or transmitted, downloaded, distributed, reverse engineered, or stored in or introduced into any information storage and retrieval system, in any form or by any means, including photocopying and recording, whether electronic or mechanical, now known or hereinafter invented without permission in writing from the publisher.

Dorrance Publishing Co
585 Alpha Drive
Pittsburgh, PA 15238
Visit our website at www.dorrancebookstore.com

ISBN: 978-1-4809-9045-6
eISBN: 978-1-4809-9067-8

TABLE OF CONTENTS

Chapter 1: The Secret Dome Room 1

Chapter 2: Bud 5

Chapter 3: Dawn 11

Chapter 4: Group 21

Chapter 5: Under the Stairs 27

Chapter 6: Who's Who 31

Chapter 7: Revelation 39

Chapter 8: The Letter 53

Chapter 9: Planning a Valentine's Day Surprise 57

Chapter 10: Time to Go 63

Chapter 11: Martha 67

Chapter 12: Ali's Life and Regrets 73

Chapter 13: A Friend in Joy 87

Chapter 14: Getting to Know You 91

Chapter 15: Can We Talk? 95

Chapter 16: Homecoming 101

Chapter 17: Therapy Begins 109
Chapter 18: The Awakening 117
Chapter 19: The Visitor 133
Chapter 20: Community 145
Chapter 21: Unity 149
Chapter 22: Bonus Weekend 167
Chapter 23: Road Trip 183
Chapter 24: The Welcome 193
Chapter 25: Conclusion 201

Introduction

The dome was located in St. Louis, MO in the very middle of the country. This is where many of the mentally ill were treated. It was a sprawling complex with many out buildings where the clients resided. The residential areas were newer-looking brick structures that were all surrounded by high steel and wrought iron fencing. The building that housed the dome was used for individual therapy, group therapy, and training rooms that were all on the lower level. The next couple of floors were all for administrative services. To get to the dome, you had to take an elevator that went to the fifth floor and then walk the last two flights of stairs to the heavy steel door leading into the great rounded room. The room measured about 40 feet in diameter with the entrance coming out right in the middle of the room. The maintenance men had long ago started storing the old files in cabinets up there. The desks were empty, and the dome room was not used for anything anymore. It would have made a wonderful lunch room or gathering room for a staff get-together at one time long ago, but now it was all but deserted. Large windows provided much light during the day with sunsets that were actually quite pictorial, considering the assortment of views from the surrounding area. It was a city that was always busy, with its people always hustling in a hurry to go who knows where, to, or from and never just being leisurely. Hundreds of cars drove past the iron gates daily that housed the hospital with its picturesque grounds, inviting, yet intimidating guard shack, and of course, the magnificent turquoise dome. The population that surrounded the hospital were as diverse as the people within.

Snow at The Dome

One lonely person that knew the Dome better than most now rode the train. It was unrealistically quiet as Dr. Sunn rode across the country's heartland, distancing himself hundreds of miles away from the Dome. But Dr. Sunn could not distance himself from the long treatments and years of meetings and sessions he had with Snow, Bud, Baby Girl, Aunty Kay, Dawn, Hope, and yes, Patty. These events continued to play in his head as current events. He allowed his mind to go back there to the extreme chaotic nightmare that had been ignited by a stranger and entity from a foreign place. This man was in truth the enemy, not just his, he thought. He arrived on our soil with a hostile perspective and with a preconceived disregard for our way of life and animosity for the female gender. He felt his own thoughts beginning to get cluttered in his mind again. He heard himself say aloud, "Stop!"

He felt he had interchanged myriads of fantasies, horrors, and heartbreak. It was a test, he thought, of my own mental endurance and sanity itself. School had taught Dr. Sunn many things before he started practicing clinical psychotherapy, but no matter how many lessons, how many practice sessions, how many long hours into the nights reading books on early childhood trauma and personality development, nothing was to properly prepare him for his time with Snow. And in all truthfulness, he was grateful because the other side, the reward side, had given him the opportunity to act as Snow's therapist.

He looked outside of his window, his eyes locked on the amber waves of grain, there they were, right outside his dining car window, waving to him. He could not demise if they were waving goodbye or come back. They beckoned him to a place of peace. But his thoughts went anywhere but where they might make sense. He attempted to think about his old classmates, instructors, professors, colleagues, family, but his thoughts all kept going back to Snow. He was having a hard time separating feeling from fantasy. Human torture has no bounds, and he was struggling to understand the depth of depravity.

The destination for the ride was eventually to end with the meeting of old friends. He thought of what he might say or proclaim then. But for now, the purchase of an open-ended ticket gave him the ability to stop and start again from most anywhere. Time alone to shift through the scenes and words playing in his mind. I'll start again when the value of the stop fades, then I will move on, and I will arrive in time, Dr. Sunn thought to himself. Then, as he closed his eyes, his mind went back to Snow.

Chapter One

The Secret Dome Room Meeting

He first saw her in the chronic ward, 'the land of the lost,' as staff described it. The unit with poor souls that had lost their minds. But no one really called her lost, not even then. They called her the sweet one. Her chart read selective mutism and catatonic. She spent hours alone in her room, drawing and painting beautiful pictures, and never uttering a single word. Selective mutism described her, after all, she had not opened up to anyone or even had a conversation with anyone he knew of for at least one year. But she opened up to him the first time he saw her. Dr. Sunn thought to himself, It wasn't with words, though, it was that swift quick smile that turned up at the sides of her mouth. It was only a fraction of a second, but I knew! I saw it, he thought to himself, we connected. I remembered seeing her name on the chart, Snow DuTro. I looked into Snow's green eyes, I really saw her, and I was able to glimpse deep into her soul, he thought. He remembered that Snow sat there, not moving, just frozen in the room, and he remembered knowing then that underneath her silence was life. Her eyes told him, "I need your help," and her smile confirmed that transference had occurred, and they had made a connection. He agreed to take her case on. He knew he had awoken her. That type of work isn't done by just an average man, he thought.

Once Snow came out of her psychotic state, she was able to roam the campus, and she discovered every nook and cranny. She would often hide out in a secret place for days. The staff would frantically look for her, but they were never able to find her or to find her hideaway. She would always just turn back up after a few days. The treatment she had undergone had taught her well. She also had paid close attention to her therapy. She knew the therapeutic process. She could speak the jargon, she knew how to resist and how to lead a therapist on. But Dr. Sunn thought to himself, "I broke in. I was able to go into her world and bring her out."

After working with Snow for months, he found himself standing on the bottom of a stairway. He looked up at the metal winding staircase that led up to the room in the top of the dome. His hand tightly gripped the railing. He held the railing, taking hold of the future while standing in the past. He knew she was at the top of the stairs in the dome. She would be waiting for him in the vast empty room furnished only with the eight chairs. Dr. Sunn inhaled deeply, the air filling his lungs with oxygen. Dr. Sunn was a man in his late 20's. Not tall in physical stature, nor was he by any means what someone might call muscular. He thought of himself as being average, but he knew he was a gifted therapist.

Dr. Sunn started to ascend the stairs. The stairs seem to move slightly underneath his weight, and with each step, they made a metallic, echoing sound, letting Snow know he was on his way. Just like the first time, her first group! He knew his steps had alerted the group in session. He was on his way up, making his way into Snow's world. He thought back to the first night he saw the faint glow of the dome six months prior.

It was late that night he remembered how quiet the campus had seemed. Most people were sleeping except for the night shift. He was heading for his car that night when he looked up and saw the room aglow. He had walked across campus and climbed the winding stairs to open the door and find Snow. Snow had yelled at him to come in. Then Snow introduced him to the seven other group members; Bud, Baby Girl, Dawn, Louie, Auntie Kay, and Hope. Then he watched Snow sitting in her chair, smiling, as she led 'her' group. He thought then he should close the group down, but he didn't. He let it continue.

The first session, he was not invited to attend. Snow arranged everything herself without consulting him. Even though Snow had been admitted in a catatonic state, he knew she definitely was aware of her surroundings. She knew more about the hospital and the grounds than the Head of Psychiatrics, Dr. Rose, did.

As Dr. Sunn reached the door at the top of the stairs, Snow called out, just as she had done the night of the initial session.

"Come on in, Dr. Sunn, we have been waiting for you. Did you remember that Bud is graduating tonight? He is leaving us!"

Dr. Sunn sat there, reflecting to the first time he was introduced to Bud. It was the second night of Snow's group when he had entered the dome room with doubts. Now, after six months, he thought, what progress, Bud is leaving because he had let the group continue.

Dr. Sunn thought to himself, Snow has made progress, but I will not take the credit. I am just the catalyst to bring about the possibility of change. No, if I take the credit, I will also carry the blame. No thanks! But now, Bud is leaving the group. Wow! Could it be? Just six months ago was the first time he was introduced, if he could call it an introduction. It was more like an attack." Thinking back, he remembered, "I had just stuck my head in the door of the secret dome room when Bud screamed out, startling me.

"Hello, Dr. Sunn," came a loud high-pitched voice. "My name is Bud. Not sure what they said about me or if they told you my diagnosis, but I'm kind of wild and can't sit still. I have always been the class clown."

After regaining his composure, the somewhat shocked Dr. Sunn decided just to go with it, to follow the flow, so he asked Bud, "Do you lose things, do you feel driven, and do you space-out a lot?"

"That's me," Bud said in that shrill voice.

Dr. Sunn just nodded his head as an acknowledgement. Snow responded with an understanding look.

"Well, it sounds to me like ADHD."

"Yeah, Dr. Sunn, that's what Snow said, I was ADHD or attention something or other. Didn't she tell you that?"

"Well, Bud, no. I haven't really had the chance to talk with anyone, and I cannot diagnose without giving you an assessment."

"No need, doc, I got you," Bud said as he was fidgeting, tapping his feet, and looking all around the room but never fixing his eyes on anything for long. His hands grasped the sides of his chair tightly as if he were trying to pick himself up and walk with his chair.

Chapter Two

Bud

"Let's start the meeting by examining prior history," said Dr. Sunn. "Snow, will you please tell the group how you and Bud first met?"

"It was a long time ago, way before I got sick," Snow said as she was staring down at the floor with a thoughtful look on her face. "It was the night of the pizza. I remember I had to beg my father to let me order a pizza. My father was an introverted person, he was isolated from society, and he kept me in the house. We had a huge house, but we all lived kind of separate and lonely lives. Our house was surrounded by a wall with a security gate. I was not able to go out like other kids. I never could go to anyone's house, and no one was ever able to come to my house. I never had a sleepover. My father was so strict, he or my Aunt Joy drove me to school and picked me up as soon as school was over. I could never belong to Girl Scouts or after school clubs or anything like that. It was me and my father and my Aunt Joy. It was like being in prison and Joy was my guard. Whenever I complained or asked for things to be different, they would always respond in the same way, 'It is Allah's will, or it is written!' My father was a Muslim, and my Aunt Joy who was the first wife of his brother, she was an American and a Muslim advocate."

"My mom was there, I suppose, but she was always sick, always in bed. My mother lived in a separate area in the house. She ate her meals and spent her entire day and night in there alone. I can only remember glimpses of her here and there. I'm starting to remember a lot more about things though. Bud has helped me, he has always been a friend in need, I do remember that. I also remember thinking if the world came to an end, I would want Bud there. He has a way of making me laugh. And the pizza night might have felt like the end of the world, but Bud was there!"

"That night was rare. When I remember my father, I remember a warden: strict, ungiven and unyielding. But that night was different. My father was in a good mood, which was not like him at all," Snow said with a little giggle. "He had had a couple of beers that night, and my mother was better that night, too. She had taken her medicine without a big fight, at least that's what I thought. Anyway, I had been begging probably for at least six months for my father to please let me order a pizza. All the kids in school had told me about pizza. They had told me how it was made from dough and how there was melted cheese on it and how it tasted so good. They bragged about how they were able to order one. I thought it sounded like a 'right-of-passage' or something like that. So that night, my father said I could order one. He went to the closet and unlocked the door and took out the phone and the phone book. I rarely had a chance to look at the phone book. It usually remained hidden and locked away by dear, old father," she continued as she stared straight out into the vast room. "I remember he told me to pick a pizza parlor out and then to call the pizza place and order a large cheese pizza with mushrooms, green peppers and onions. So, I did and then I waited anxiously for the pizza to arrive. I heard the alarm for the security gate, I went to the monitor and buzzed him in. I heard a car drive up, and I was able to look out of the tightly shaded window and see a car. I saw a yellow light on the top of the car, and I could see the writing on it said, 'Pizza.'"

"I remember I had just reached the door to buzz the gate open. I was ready to hand the delivery boy my money and to bring in that wonderful pizza when I heard a lot of commotion. It was coming from the stairway. My mom had made it halfway down the stairs. As I looked over my shoulder, I could see that glazed look in my mother's eyes, her long hair was a massive mess, sticking up everywhere all over on her head, so unruly. My mom was very ill. I looked, and I could see her mouth was starting to open. I knew she was going to scream. I knew it was going to be one of those horrible moments when I became so embarrassed and ashamed because of my mother. She was just so crazy at times. My father had told me many times that my mom was ill, mentally ill. It was always dreadful when my father had to intervene physically with my mom, but my father was able to intervene again that night. He was able to put his big hand over her mouth and wrap his arm around her, pulling her back up the stairs. The timing was so right that night. My father dragged my mother back up the stairs out of sight. At that very moment, the pizza delivery boy was at the door. I rushed over to answer the door. He was handing me the liter of Pepsi, but as I took it from him, I dropped it. It hit the ceramic floor so hard that it started spraying Pepsi all over the kitchen as the bottle spun in circles. The delivery boy had tried to grab the bottle of Pepsi, but he slipped and started to fall. I reached out to grab him, but I was slipping and sliding in the Pepsi also, my arms started waving all around, and I knocked that pizza out of the delivery boys other hand as we both went down. What a mess! My father heard all the commotion on his way back from upstairs. As he walked into the kitchen, he was very calm, and his presence demanded a sense of calmness in the room. He reached down and pulled me up, standing me firmly back on my feet. He then extended his hand to the delivery boy and pulled him up. My father apologized to the delivery boy as he reached into his pocket and pulled out a hundred-dollar bill. He stuffed it into the delivery boy's hand. My father then turned around and barked out an order to me to take care of the mess. Then he added, 'Before your Aunt Joy sees it,' as he slowly and purposely walked back up the stairs."

"The kitchen door was still open as the delivery boy made his quick exit. I slowly closed the door, feeling bad. That was the first time I saw Bud. He was rather cute, this guy hiding behind the door with a big ridiculous looking smile! I remember thinking, how out of place this seemed. For this guy to be there, smiling with this big grin on his face after what had just happened. Bud came in the kitchen during the chaos and somehow hid himself behind the open door. I couldn't even ask him who he was before he went into this hysterical laughter. He laughed so hard, I began to laugh, too. We ended up in one of those laughing fits. We tried so hard to stop, but it was that kind of laughing that hurts your sides so bad. My sides were killing me, but we just could not stop it. After at least five minutes of laughing, we were able to catch our breath. That's when Bud introduced himself to me as the neighbor. I started to apologize, but that is when Bud stopped me. He wouldn't let me. He told me that was the funniest thing he had ever seen and that he was so glad that he was able to witness that. Then he added that he wanted to hang out with me more, so that we can laugh and have more fun as he continued to smile at me with that ridiculous grin. I explained to Bud that my father was very secluded and strict. And that he didn't even allow me to have friends. Bud told me that was okay and that he was a good sneak and he'd see me again."

"I'll just watch, I'll get another chance when the gates are opened."

Then Bud left as I closed the door and began to clean up the mess. The pizza was smashed and covered with Pepsi, I remember thinking, too bad I wasn't even able to have even one slice of pizza, but I now had a new friend!

"My father would never let me order pizza again. It's kind of sad, but the first time I ever tasted pizza was here at the institution. But Bud had become my friend, and he would always show up just in time for me, as he still does." Snow smiled and turned her head toward Bud's chair. "Only amazing people can find humor in difficult situations," she said, "you're amazing, Bud."

"Hey, Dr. Sunn," piped up Bud. "I took it upon myself to order a pizza for this night to celebrate my departure from the group."

"I think that is very fitting, Bud" said Dr. Sunn.

Just then, the pizza was delivered. "Come on, Dr. Sunn, let's get our slice of the pie," Bud said.

As they sat eating their pizza, Bud thanked Dr. Sunn for all he had done for him during the last several months. Dr. Sunn watched Bud as he tore off the pepperoni, piece by piece, and threw it up in the air, snatching it, and gulping each piece down one by one. Each just in the nick of time, thought Dr. Sunn. "Hey, Bud, your timing is so precise."

"That's right, Dr. Sunn. My timing is like a gift. I'm like a fine running clock, I've been wound just tight enough."

"Tell me more about that, Bud," said Dr. Sunn.

Bud started to laugh. "No, I'm done with that psycho stuff, but save it, Dr. Sunn. You are going to need it."

"What do you mean?" asked Dr. Sunn.

"Just between you and me," Bud whispered, "I made my decision to leave about a week ago."

"Oh, I see," said Dr. Sunn, sitting back in his chair and taking a deep breath.

"That's right," said Bud, "it was the day you and Snow and some of the other patients were playing that card game in the lounge. The game where you stick the cards behind your head and hold them up, so everyone else knows your hand but you."

"I remember that day, Bud. They call that game the Blind Man's Bluff."

"Well," said Bud, "that's the day I knew it was time for me to leave the group. Snow was laughing so hard that day, she was genuinely happy. She was having such a time, Dr. Sunn, that is when I heard the clock within me chime, and I knew I was going to move on! It was like

Snow did not need me anymore, I was free. Does that make sense to you, Dr. Sunn?"

"Yes, it does, Bud," said Dr. Sunn. "But what did you mean when you said I was going to need it?"

"Oh," said Bud. "I'm like a clock, but that crazy girl, Dawn, she is a nut, and unlike me, she is going to be hard to crack! She's been sneaking out of the hospital some nights. There's no telling where she has been going. I've tried to get her to talk, but she is just crazy. Today, I thought she might tell me because she knows I'm leaving. I figure she would know that I'm not a threat. But she wouldn't tell me. She just put that bright red lip stick on and smacked her lips together, laughing. Well, Dr. Sunn, it's time for me to leave. I have to go tell all the others goodbye. Hope you enjoyed the pizza! After all, the hospitals paying for it, it came out of the community fund."

Dr. Sunn just sat there. I'm glad it's Friday, he thought.

Chapter Three

Dawn

Monday morning, while Dr. Sunn stood looking out of his office window and appreciating the beautiful scenery, he thought about how the campus was changed into almost a magical land with the freshly fallen snow. He was admiring the evergreen trees that were covered in white, they shone brightly when gently touched by rays from the sun.

Snow did her disappearing act again and hid out for two days. Staff was not able to find her Saturday or Sunday; those are good days to misbehave. The hospital is a different world during the weekends. Regular staff is off, and sessions are not conducted. Dr. Sunn thought, we need to change her coping mechanism. Just then, she reappeared for her therapy session.

"'Here I am, Dr. Sunn. The nurse told me you were looking for me."

"Snow, please stop disappearing! Where have you been hiding? You haven't had your meds. Just come on in and talk to me. You've been gone for two days."

"I'm sorry, Dr. Sunn. I just feel overwhelmed. Really, I don't do it on purpose," Snow said with her head down.

"Well, we need to cut this session short," Dr. Sunn continued. "Staff needs to document that you were found and administer your medication."

"Really sorry, Dr. Sunn," said Snow. "I will let you know next time I feel like hiding."

"Is that a promise?" Dr. Sunn asked with a stern look as he rang for the nurse to come for Snow.

Yes, Snow's initial breakthrough had been costly and somewhat dangerous, he thought. It was as if she had regressed to when she first came out of the catatonic state. In those days, she would hide out on the campus for days. Staff would do their best to find her, but no one ever did. She would just show up, either in the med line, in the cafeteria, in her room, or just walk in to a scheduled session like nothing had happened. When asked about her disappearance, she would act as if she didn't know what the staff was talking about. She just went on as if things were normal.

A short while later, Dr. Sunn was examining a map of the hospital and the many diverse buildings on campus. Where is her hide out and how can she be gone for days? But his thoughts were disrupted when he heard a loud commotion. He looked up in time to see his office door burst open, and before he could say anything, he heard a rich sounding woman's voice with a definite southern accent. He knew immediately who the voice he heard belonged to.

"Dr. Sunn, I'm tired of being ignored! I declare, you think you can just keep me on a shelf just like I was an old dusty antique teapot. You never have time to talk to me. I guess it is the curse of the middle child, never really seen or heard. At least that is until someone wants to find out something. That annoying Bud told me that you were wanting to have an audience with me. So, Dr. Sunn, I'm going to sit right down here in the comfy leather chair, so you can have my undivided attention." Dawn settled, shifting down deep into the folds of the over-stuffed leather chair. "So, what is it that you want to know?" asked Dawn.

Dr. Sunn looked directly into Dawn's eyes, watching for any blinking, any frowning, or any other small movement he could detect to help him analyze Dawn and her motives.

"Well, hello, Dawn. It's nice to see you, and I'm sad to hear that you feel you are being ignored. I had you on my schedule, and I had planned to talk to you during my afternoon rounds today. I thought you might know something about who paid for the pizza for Bud's good-bye party. Bud had mentioned it came out of the hospitals community funds, but I looked at the books this morning and there weren't any withdrawals."

"Dr. Sunn, why would you think I know anything about any pizza money?" Dawn said as she held on to the edge of the chair.

"Dawn, are you missing that little glittered clutch purse that usually is attached to your wrist by a little strap?" asked Dr. Sunn.

"Well now, let me think about that, hmmmm, yes, I do declare that I have not seen my purse for a day or so. Why are you so interested that I misplaced my purse? I don't get it, Dr. Sunn."

"I thought it might interest you, Dawn," Dr. Sunn replied, "to learn that a small glittered clutch purse was turned in to me by nurse Vicki. Nurse Vicki also stated that there was over $100 in singles and five-dollar bills stuffed into that tiny purse. And upon opening the purse, I verified her statement was true. I was going to inform you that your purse was found and ask if you had lost it or if you knew anything about how that much money got into your purse."

"Dr. Sunn, are you accusing me of stashing money in my purse?" she asked. "Where would I get any money from? I think that you may be delusional."

"Dawn, we have already confirmed several facts," he continued. "One being that your purse is missing and two, that your missing purse looks exactly like the glittered purse that nurse Vicki turned in to me this morning. Also, Dawn, there have been reports that you have been leaving the hospital grounds at night."

"Dr. Sunn, I will not be interrogated. I have no idea what the hell you are talking about, and I never said that that was my purse. I merely stated mine was missing. Someone must have taken it and stuffed it full of bills!"

"That's a very interesting theory, Dawn," he said. "Would Freud call that reverse psychology?"

"Dr. Sunn, the only thing I know about Freud is what he said about sex and that sex messes people up. And he came to that fact long before he even knew anybody in Snow's group. Dr. Sunn, I do not believe in love. I believe in selfish sex. I don't think love exists. I think people want to gratify their own selfish desires. So, I admit I'm selfish."

"Dawn," Dr. Sunn started as he was clearing his voice, "what correlation is there between sex and that money in your purse?"

Dawn was up and gone, slamming the door before Dr. Sunn could ask the next question. "Hmmm," Dr. Sunn said under his breath, "I'm going to have to talk with Snow." Dr. Sunn reached for the intercom and called the front desk. "Will you please inform Bob that I need to have a session with Snow. Ask him to escort her to my office at noon. Also, will you send me Snow DuTro's chart." Dr. Sunn sat behind his desk, connecting the dots. Dawn had mentioned sex and then Snow's group.

Just then, Nurse Vicky walked in.

"Here you go, Dr. Sunn. This chart is huge. It is the thickest chart I've seen!" she said as she handed it to him.

Dr. Sunn was still viewing Snow's chart when Bob the orderly knocked on his office door. "Here she is, doc!"

"Hello, Snow, I was just reviewing your chart. Come on in and have a seat."

Snow smiled at Dr. Sunn as she took a seat in the big leather chair.

"I thought we should finish our session that was cut short. I think it is time we had a one on one. It says here that you arrived here in a cab. The cabby said he just followed instructions given him by his dispatcher. Still no memories?"

Snow shook her head no.

He continued, "It also reads that you were on narcotics. We think that you overdosed and that is why you were in a coma. When the cabby was questioned, he said he had picked you up on a corner. He could not give an address, and it says here that he thought that the person who called and paid for the cab knew you really needed to be here. There was no missing person report, nothing to follow up on. No one, including Dr. Rose, has been able to figure out the mystery."

"Snow," he said, "usually when I read a chart, it helps to clarify things. But your chart only leads to more mysteries. So, let's move on, but please, Snow, let me know about any memories that might surface."

"Yes, I will Dr. Sunn," she answered. "I do want to remember more."

He went on, "I had wanted to use this session to focus on your past and your memories, but before we get too deep into that, we need to talk about Dawn." Redirecting, Dr. Sunn said, "Let's focus on the group and perceptibly Dawn. Snow, do you know what's going on with Dawn?"

"Dr. Sunn, I'm not aware of anything that's going on with Dawn. Why?" she asked.

Dr. Sunn explained his prior meeting with Dawn.

"I see" said Snow, "but I really don't have a clue."

"Okay, okay, Snow. I would like you to do a favor for me. Will you draw the group for me, so I can see how you see them? I would like more insight into their characters. I feel you could give me that in your descriptions."

"Well, that's kind of a funny thing to ask me, but okay," she replied. "I'm told I'm a very good artist. After all, art is my thing! I have always been drawing and painting pictures since I woke up from the coma. Dr. Sunn, for all you have done for me, I will give it my best shot."

"We've been through quite a lot together, Snow. I knew we could be a great team and make progress," he concluded.

"Dr. Sunn, I need to thank you for giving me a second chance here. It was you that convinced Dr. Rose to agree to take me off the Haldol shots. I'm so glad I have you, Dr. Sunn! I remember when I first started coming out of what staff referred to as a catatonic state. I felt lost, so confused. I feel so much better now. It's like I'm coming back from a distant place. You know, Dr. Sunn, I told you about my safe place and how beautiful it is. My safe place is all white, there is snow everywhere, but it's not cold to the touch. It feels a little chilled, like picking up a coke that's been in the refrigerator." Snow paused to look into Dr. Sunn's eyes to see if he was getting it.

Dr. Sunn smiled and nodded his head.

"And the snowflakes come in any size I want," she went on. "They can be like the ones we made in kindergarten. They are all multidimensional and multi-faceted, something like a diamond, but they remain white. They can be enormous or very tiny, almost miniscule. I can hold them and form them any way I want or blow lightly on them and watch as they just fade away. When I'm there, I feel like I'm walking on white clouds of snow. If I want to, I can fall down into the snow, sinking all the ways down into it, or I can fall on the top of it and make a snow angel. The snow is there for me. If I want to sleep, it becomes like a form fitting mattress. It can become a snowman and play with me. It's my world, and I can manipulate it anyway I want. It's always peaceful there, I'm happy there, and I'm always safe. I would have stayed there the last time I was there, but the strangest thing happened! It might have just been a dream, but Hope, our Hope from the group, came there, you know, to my safe place. She told me I had been there too long, and I needed to come back. Hope said, 'Snow, if you ever get stuck here in the future, just look for the bridge. You can get out by the bridge. Just say London Bridge is falling.'"

"Oh, I just had a new memory come into my mind," she went on. "I can remember sitting in class and making little birds and snowflakes out of construction paper."

"Snow," Dr. Sunn asked, "you say you remember making snowflakes out of paper? Was anyone else there that you can remember?"

"I remember that my teacher told me how to fold the paper and how to cut it," she answered. "I remember wanting to put it on my window at home. I can't remember anyone else but my teacher and me. It's one of those stubborn fragmental memories, just a piece, a glimpse. I don't remember where it comes from or where it's going." Snow began to cry.

"Interesting," said Dr. Sunn as he stared down at his pad, jotting something down. Looking up smiling, he said, "Good, Snow, you are starting to remember. I know your memories seem fragmented, but they will come together like a big jigsaw puzzle, you'll see." Dr. Sunn put his arm around Snow, patting her on the back for comfort.

"Some of my methods in therapy are not conventional, like the group, and letting you facilitate it." Snow tried to interrupt him, shaking her head no. He went on, "No, really, I feel I'm only a coleader and that's okay. You are making progress. And Bud graduating from the group shows me we are headed down the right path. Anyway, as I said in the beginning, I really wanted to have a session with you today, so let's talk more about your memory. Are you having more than just flashbacks here and there? It seems like you were able to recall quite a bit from the time you spent with Bud."

"Dr. Sunn, my memories are still lost, as you say," she answered. "I have repressed memories. I still can't remember a whole lot of my childhood. I can't even remember the beginning of my stay here. My mind is like watching one of those old films, it flicks in and out. A face, a room, a smell, and then sometimes the whole incident comes back or sometimes I can remember days. Like I said, I remember wanting to tape that snowflake to my window and then nothing. I do have a memory though that keeps surfacing. It's when I'm setting on a soft blue rug. I remember my mom's face, but she didn't have that hysterical look I usually remember her having, and we are looking down at some kind of light, then the memory is gone!"

"Snow, I was going through your chart right before you came in, and I came across something very interesting," Dr. Sunn told her. "A detail that seemed important. When you first came to the hospital, it was noted that you were wearing a blue coat. Your chart explains it very well. It had a white furry collar, and there was a label sewn into it with your name on it, Snow DuTro. That is how staff was able to identify you. I thought you might like me to get that coat out of property, it might bring back some memories."

"I would like that very much, Dr. Sunn," she said, "and I want to thank you again for all you have done for me. I wish I could help you more with Dawn, but I'm really at a loss."

"That's okay, Snow," he reassured her. "That was a great session. We did some productive work. Snow, do you think I could talk to Dawn further?"

"I'll see if I can go and find her. Bye for now, Dr. Sunn," Snow said as she walked out of the office.

Looking up from his desk, Dr. Sunn saw Dawn standing there. "Well, hello, Dawn. You left the office so abruptly, we weren't able to finish our session."

"I didn't know that was a therapy session Dr. Sunn," she told him. "I thought I was just being interrogated!"

"Dawn," he said, "I guess I'm just going to have to take you by your word and believe you when you tell me you don't know anything about that purse or it being filled with over a hundred dollars and that you are truthful. I have to ask myself, why would you keep something like that from me, your therapist? So, moving on, we'll just have to explore in depth how a purse that looks exactly like your purse ended up here at the hospital with all that money in it tonight at group. Maybe another group member will have some insight."

"Lordy me, Dr. Sunn, are you fixing on making my life completely miserable or what?" she sarcastically asked. "If you bring it up in group tonight, Aunty Kay is going to lose it. You know how she has to have control over everything. She thinks she's the 'grand protector.' We all love Snow, but she is really overly possessive. I'll make a deal with you, if you just forget about this purse thing, I will do some analytic work with you. I'll sit right here in this chair right now and let you analyze me. I'll even talk to you about my past and the abuse I suffered and what I witnessed. Deal, Dr. Sunn?"

"Yes, Dawn, we have a deal," Dr. Sunn agreed. "Let's plan on us having an individual session tomorrow. I plan on being in group tonight, and we will keep this between ourselves for now. Oh, I did mention this to Snow, but she needs to know. She is really the group leader."

"That sounds like a dandy plan," Dawn said as she left the office.

Chapter Four

Group

That night, Dr. Sunn stood at the door to the group room. He took a deep breath and thought to himself, this is going to be a revealing group session. He then stepped into his role of co-leader of Snow's amazing group. He was met with Snow's bright, shining smile.

"Dr. Sunn, I drew the group like you asked me to do," she told him right away.

"Wow, Snow, that looks pretty good!" he told her.

"I really enjoyed doing it. I used the mindful technique you taught us. Okay," said Snow, "this is our first meeting without Bud, I really miss him already. I thought we could use this time to acknowledge his achievements and to clarify why we are here and what each of our goals are. Dr Sunn, will you continue, I'm feeling overwhelmed with Bud's absence." With a saddened face, Snow bowed her head.

"Okay, as I sit here among this group," Dr. Sunn began, "I am looking at a picture Snow has drawn of all of you. Bud is in the drawing also. I'm impressed with her perspective and the way she sees all of you. So, as I go around the room and call out your name, I will comment on Snow's perception of each of you. Baby Girl, Snow shows you as being withdrawn. You are standing looking down with slumped shoulders.

Your face looks like an angel. So, Baby Girl, why are you here tonight, and why did you want to belong to this group? What do you want to achieve?"

With a tiny voice and with poor pronunciation and a slight stutter, it made it hard to understand what Baby Girl was saying, but she was able to say, "I'm here because Snow asked me to come. And I really love her, and I wanted to make her happy."

"But why are you here for yourself?" Dr. Sunn asked her. "What has happened that you find yourself here today, in this group?"

"Oh, because the uncle hurt me, and the father gave me to him. I was a child bride. I want to feel good about myself, and I do not want to feel scared anymore when I talk to other people." With that, Baby Girl quickly sat back down.

"Very good, Baby Girl," he told her. "Dawn, you're next. As I look at this picture, you look very excited, smiling, and waving your hand. Your makeup and your hair expertly done. You look like a model that just stepped down the runway."

"Thank you, Dr. Sunn. You're such a gentleman," she replied. "I just want to say, of course, that I'm here because Snow asked me to come. Also, I saw a man sexually abuse Snow's mother over and over and over. I want to bring some light on who Snow's mother was and what she suffered."

"STOP! STOP!" yelled Aunty Kay. "This is all ridiculous, Baby Girl and Dawn are not putting the responsibility where it belongs."

Dr. Sunn could see that Aunty Kay was escalating. "Aunty Kay, please calm down."

Aunty Kay went on, "Their mothers, the mother that was unable to protect them, is to blame. Their mothers are psychotic bitches just like Snow's mom. Hell, that's why we're all here, we all love Snow and we want to help her, but I am not participating in this masquerade. Let's just say we all had messed up mothers and that we had to deal with their shit."

"How dare you judge good mothers!" yelled Dawn.

"Missy, you need to sit back down and shut your mouth," yelled Aunty Kay.

Dawn, jumping up red-faced with tight angry lips, began to yell, "You're a control freak, a liar, and a mean person. I'm tired of you and your threats always shutting everyone down. Why don't you and your dog Louie come over here and try to shut my mouth. I'll kick both of your asses and shut you both up!" screamed Dawn.

Dr. Sunn stood up, hoping to draw Snow's attention and to calm the group down. The next thing Dr. Sunn saw were chairs and a table being thrown. Louie was out of control. Dr. Sunn wrestled him down and used his pager. Soon, an orderly was rushing into the room and was about to administer a shot of Thorazine when Dr. Sunn shouted, "That won't be necessary," as he continued to restrain Louie. Dr. Sunn felt Louie going limp. "Louie!" he yelled, "are you still here?" Louie fought within himself to stay and gained control of himself. After a few minutes passed, Dr. Sunn said, "Louie, I'm going to let you go. Are you calm?"

"Yes, I am, I'm okay now," responded the shaken Louie.

Dr. Sunn slowly released Louie. Needless to say, the group ended for the night.

Later the same night of the disruptive group, Aunty Kay met with Louie privately back in the dome.

"Hush now, let's keep it down so we are not overheard," whispered Aunty Kay. "Louie, something is going on with Dawn, and we have been kept in the dark. I need you to, no, I order you to follow Dawn and watch her every step," said Aunty Kay.

So, Louie obeyed his orders and followed Dawn. He followed her down to a side of town that Dawn described as the side of town where the party never ends.

He watched Dawn as she entered a side door of a small building. Once inside, she disappeared into the dressing room. She came out dressed in an outfit that sparsely covered her. Louie thought it looked like she was wearing a small bikini that glittered. As she approached the stairs, screams, shrills, and applause went up. Dawn took to the stage like she owned it. Once the music started to play, she began her dance, sexually swaying back and forth to the music. The audience began to throw money to her. Some of them would stuff it under a garter or in her hem. When her set was over, she gracefully walked down the stairs. She was met by a group of the patrons.

"Sam!" she yelled. We will have the $100 bottle. Dawn sat at the bar with the lucky buyer of the champagne, tossing her head back and joyfully laughing. Louie had to admit he was having a nice time himself. "This is so much better than that stinking hospital," said Louie out loud.

Dawn finished her bottle of champagne in just enough time to start her next set. Once back on stage, Dawn could easily survey the room. She could pick out the big spenders and then give them a little more attention. She liked the way she felt on stage.

She imagined herself sending mental vibes to the audience, "You can look, attempt to touch, but you can't have!" Then she spotted her friend Patti. Patti wasn't having a good night. She probably won't make anything much tonight. Just then, Dawn saw her stumble. She must have some beer in the back room, Dawn thought to herself. The girls would sneak beer in and keep it cold by putting the six pack in the back of the toilet tank, where the water ran cold. Patti must had been drinking quite a bit of beer. The drinks the bartenders gave the girls to drink didn't have alcohol in them. It was against the rules of the club for the girls dancing to really drink. Except for the $100 bottle of champagne, the only real liquor the girls were allowed. If they could lure a big spender and get a bottle of bubbly champagne, the club rewarded them, and everyone got to celebrate.

Dawn looked around and thought to herself, these girls all have serious daddy issues. What a life they live though, dancing, drinking, acting, and getting hit on. The girls were able to make the money they needed and get all of the revenge on their fathers a girl could want. Just then, Dawn saw her mark. He was a man with a wad of money and a trace of white powder on his nose. Dawn knew things were about to get a lot more interesting and fun. I'll pull Patti in with me, she thought. Together, we will be the big winners for tonight. Dawn and Patti devoted the rest of the night to partying with their newfound sugar daddy, and they showed him a really good time, one he would never forget as the debits in his bank account would remind him.

It was almost dawn as Aunty Kay stood staring out of the door, watching the grounds. Aunty Kay felt tired and thought that she might as well go get some sleep. But then she saw Dawn. Dawn was walking swiftly across the campus. She went to a side door hidden by some bushes. Aunty Kay watched as she opened the side door. Dawn quickly glanced around to ensure no one saw her right before she slipped into the entrance and disappeared.

"Got you," Aunty Kay whispered.

Louie was at Aunty Kay's door instantly, "Let me in," he insisted. Louie crept into the room. "She is going down to 17th street where she is dancing, if you want to call it that, at the Candy Apple. What a sight! The money and liquor were flowing freely. I saw her doing a line on the bar top."

"Louie, get the room ready under the stairs," said Aunty Kay. "We are going to have our first guest detained there soon. Get Dawn to go with you there before she has her session with Dr. Sunn. We can't let that session take place."

"How am I supposed to get Dawn to go with me?" Louie asked.

"Make up an excuse. Tell her that Baby Girl needs help. As a second thought," Aunty Kay added, "while I'm thinking about it, take Baby Girl there first. Show her the room, threaten her, tell her if she continues to talk, you will lock her up in there forever. Show her how you can lock down the room and remind her that no one can be heard in there, no matter what kind of racket they make. Make sure you warn her. Tell her not to tell anyone about the room or else something real bad will happen to her."

"Aunty Kay, that won't work, Baby Girl is going to tell Dawn," he said.

"No, she won't because of the father. He let something bad happen to Baby Girl. The father threatened her. He told her if she told anyone that she would get hurt real bad. He also told her that the police would take him away, and her mother would starve without anyone there to feed her."

"But that was a long time ago, right?" he asked.

"Louie, you should know," she continued. "It doesn't matter how long ago those things were said. They were a curse and a curse last as long as it replays in your head. And Baby Girl, well, she hears it every day. That is why she has a speech deficit. No, she isn't over any of it. She is still hurt and afraid. Plus, she was badly hurt. When the father gave her away, she was so badly abused, it took her a week before she stopped crying. The father must had felt bad afterward or maybe he just wanted her to shut up. Anyway, that is when he let the mother give her those dolls. Just threaten her. Tell her you are going to hurt her. She won't talk to anyone about anything, you'll see. She will just play with her dolls." Aunty Kay gave Louie a knowing nod as she smiled at him.

"I got this, Aunty Kay. I'm in charge now," Louie said. Louie laughed and swiftly disappeared as the door closed behind him.

CHAPTER FIVE

UNDER THE STAIRS

Louie stood in front of the panel that hid the heavy door to the safe room. He felt the thickness of the door with his hands as he walked into the room. Louie looked around at the beautiful furnishings and the elegant room. He saw silk veils that hung from the ceiling. The beds were also draped. The room had a slanted ceiling on the side where the stairs were constructed. Looking around, he took a deep breath. Good looking room, he thought to himself, and then began to arrange the furnishings. "This table should go here and this sofa there," Louie began to sing, "Hi-ho, hi-ho, it's off to work we go!"

Back in her room, Baby Girl was arranging her doll collection. Talking to her dolls, she was addressing them by their names. "One, you are safe, Two, you are happy, Three, you are sweet. We all will live here together and help Snow. She's our best friend."

Baby Girl, looking around the room, said, "This is a pretty dull-looking room, right, girls?" addressing her dolls. She began to laugh, "We need to bring laughter into this space, let's have some fun!" Suddenly, she heard her door open, and she gasped. "What are you doing here?"

Louie mocked Baby Girl, mocking her speech defect. "Wwwhhat aaare you ddddoing here?"

"I came to get you, Baby Girl! I'm going to take you to a safe place."

"No, I want to stay here, I'm safe here in this room with my dolls," shouted Baby Girl back at him.

"But you're not safe here," whispered Louie as he trapped her in the corner. Wrapping his arm around Baby Girl, he pulled her body toward his while he held her mouth closed, putting his left hand across her mouth. Keeping Baby Girl drawn tight to his body, he dragged her down the hallway toward the safe room. Once at the door, he put Baby Girl down. "The father is coming," he said, "and he is going to get you, Baby Girl, if you do not come into the safe room, now!"

"The safe room!" Baby Girl started to quiver and asked with a questioning look, "Do you mean the room under the stairs?"

"Yes, that's right. Let's go on in, right now," commanded Louie as he unlocked the door and gave Baby Girl a hard push.

She stumbled into the room. "What are you doing?" she yelled out. "The father is not coming, is he? I know you are lying."

"You're right, he is not coming," he told her, "but we all need to be cautious. This room is safe. It was built to withstand a bombing or a category five tornado with 200 miles an hour winds. They may beat at this door, but nothing will penetrate it. Aunty Kay and I think you are a threat to all of us. Just what did you plan on telling Dawn? Baby Girl, did you think that Aunty Kay would let you say those bad things about the father? You can't go crying to Dawn or anyone with your story about how you were hurt by the father."

"Well, Louie, during group they were asking about things," she replied. "Deep secret things, the kind we keep inside, and I feel that I have a right to tell what I saw and what happened to me. You and Aunty Kay can't stop me. I'm getting stronger! I can feel it happening, and I have decided to talk to Dawn and tell her about the bad things that happened to me. I know she needs to tell us her story, and if I tell her she might tell us what happened to her. Louie, you need to talk as well. Things have happened to you, too. You act so big and bad, but I know you were hurt. Why does Aunty Kay control you?"

"Well, Baby Girl, no one cares about what happened to you, Dawn, or me! And no one will listen. Has anyone ever listened? Besides, Aunty Kay told me to tell you not to tell anyone about what you know and what happened to you, or we will have to hurt you."

"Louie, that doesn't make any sense," she reasoned "We are supposed to talk in group, so we can all get better."

"Baby Girl, you are so stupid," he said. "If we all talk in group about things we know and things that have happened, we will just hurt each other more. So, I'm just saying this once, shut up! Just be quiet and sit there smiling or something."

"You are the one that is stupid, Louie! I want to get better, so I'm going to talk. Now leave me out of this room!" demanded Baby Girl. "Or I will scream."

Louie blocked the doorway with his body and then slipped out, shutting the door behind him, leaving Baby Girl alone and scared. Louie then opened up the slanted window, and getting close, he said, "Go ahead and yell, no one will hear you, Baby Girl." Louie began to run down the hallway, trying to get to Aunty Kay as fast as he could. As he turned the corner, he ran right into Dawn.

"Why are you running, Louie, what's the matter?" asked Dawn.

"Uh, I was on my way to get Aunty Kay, what are you doing?" he asked.

"Well, I have a session with Dr. Sunn, and I am late," she told him.

Louie quickly decided to grab the opportunity at hand. Reaching out, he quickly grabbed Dawn's arm and said, "Come with me, now."

"Leave go of me," said Dawn as she tugged at her arm.

"No," Louie said, "come with me if you want to help Baby Girl."

"Why, what happened with Baby Girl?" asked Dawn.

"She is stuck, and she needs your help bad. I was going to get Aunty Kay, but I don't have time, so you can come with me now."

"Okay, okay just let go of my arm," she told him.

"Hurry!" yelled Louie as he hustled Dawn down the corridor toward the safe room.

Chapter Six

Who's Who

Dr. Sunn sat at his desk, writing his note, thinking and going over the events and the mayhem that occurred at Snow's last group. The group was out of control, he thought to himself, but I know we're on the threshold of a breakthrough. Second thinking himself, he then thought, maybe I should just shut it down. Most therapists would have shut it down the first night. It has to be shut down, he thought. But then his mind went to Snow. No, how could he not continue to make progress. He had worked so hard, Snow had worked so hard also. Even though he knew it was painful for her at times. He turned his mind to the thought that any group takes on a life of its own, and a successful group has to run in its own schema. And after all, Snow seemed so confident, and we are making progress. And hadn't Snow been in control during all of the other sessions? But then what happened at that last session, and how in the hell did Louie end up in control? "Stop!" He heard himself exclaim.

He then said out loud to himself, "No! I will allow the group to continue," and then he ended his note with, this group will resume and will continue to warp into its own unique life. His final thought about the group was that if he had learned one thing about the mind, it was that the reality of the world is negotiated in the individual mind.

Looking at the clock, he realized it was past time for the session. Hmm, where is Dawn? he thought. She had made it known to me that she needed to be seen for an individual session, and now she's 15 minutes late. Dr. Sunn had no idea of what was going on in the safe room at that very moment or that Aunty Kay had asserted herself trying to control the other group members. And to her own and everyone else's peril, neither did Snow. How far and deep did the group members need to go into their own worlds, and would they be able to accept reality?

Dr. Sunn knew that something was going on as he sat there going over and over things in his mind, and he kept going back to the purse. And why did Dawn have that big upset when questioned? Dr. Sunn reached for the intercom and called the front desk. "Will you please inform Bob that I need to have a session with Snow. Ask him to escort her to my office right away, please!" Then he quickly added a thank you as he released the button on his phone pad.

As Dr. Sunn waited for Snow, he pushed back his chair and then thoughtfully strolled toward the closet door in his office. Is Snow ready? he asked himself. He had pushed hard during her last individual session. She was remembering, she is ready, he thought. He opened the door and pulled out the soft blue coat. Walking back toward his desk, he opened the bottom drawer and folding the coat up neatly, he laid it nicely inside the drawer, then sat back down.

Meanwhile, the participants of Snow's group were moving toward self-awareness. Louie was standing in front of the safe room door with Dawn.

"Louie, why is Baby Girl in the safe room, and what is going on here?" asked Dawn.

"You will see," said Louie as he opened the door slowly, then quickly shoving Dawn through the door. Dawn looked around and saw the gorgeous room that was 16' by 20'. It was beautiful marble inlaid flooring with the added luxury of thick Persian carpets. The walls were done in exquisite murals exhibiting beautiful locations throughout the world. Cedar was used as trim. The heavy door was also sound proof with only a hidden, small double glass window that allowed light in.

Louie locked the door and opened the small window. He peered in through the slanted window, shaking his head back and forth. "Aunty Kay wanted to shut you up, Dawn, and now, I'm locking you both up."

Baby Girl stood in the corner crying, "I need my dolls!"

"For heaven sakes," yelled Dawn at Louie. "You need to at least get her dolls! You know she has always had them with her since the beginning."

"I will do nothing else until I can talk with Aunty Kay first," he responded.

"Does she know what you have done? Did Aunty Kay tell you to do this?" yelled Dawn.

"I-I-I-I-I," stuttered Louie. "Why ask me that?"

"Because," replied Dawn. "You can't do anything without her okaying it first. If you did this without her permission, you will bring us all down. I know that Aunty Kay would not separate Baby Girl from her dolls."

Louie closed the slanted window and swiftly walked away in search of Aunty Kay.

• • • • •

Back in his office, Dr. Sunn's thoughts were disturbed by Bob's knocking at the door.

"Here we are. Sorry, Dr. Sunn," said Bob, "but I had a hard time waking Snow up. Here she is," Bob said as he turned and left.

Snow entered the office. Dr. Sunn smiled up at Snow, "Have a seat. Snow, have you talked with Dawn?"

"No, I haven't seen her yet," she answered.

"She had wanted an individual session with me," he continued. "She made it seem like it was important to her."

"No, Dr. Sunn, I haven't talked with her since the group."

"Will you try to find her and send her to my office once we're done?" he asked.

"Yes, I will tell her," Snow replied in a soft low tone.

"Snow, since you're here, we should have our daily session. Snow, I think the group is a good thing for you, but I have some concerns," Dr. Sunn went on to say. "During the last group, things got away from you and you lost control." He cleared his throat, then continued. "Snow, groups have a way of taking on their own direction. Members can often behave different than expected when they are in a group setting. I really have some concerns, and I actually had to talk myself into letting the group resume."

"Yeah, I know," Snow said. "Aunty Kay scared me when she started yelling and then Louie got aggressive. I felt bad for all of us but mostly for Baby Girl and Dawn. But, Dr. Sunn, I can control it. I want to have group tonight. I feel that tonight we need to support Baby Girl and Dawn and to put some boundaries in for the others."

"Okay, Snow," he told her. "I have given this a lot of thought, and I'll agree if you can guarantee you can control the group tonight."

"I've got this, Dr. Sunn," she assured him.

"Okay, Snow. Then we are doing group tonight. Did you bring your drawing?" he asked.

Shaking her head yes, she smiled and handed Dr. Sunn the last of her three drawings.

"Snow, you are a talented artist," he said as he studied the drawings. "Talk to me about your drawings and give me more of your insight into each one."

"Okay," she said as she pointed to the drawing she had done of Hope. "That is the way I see Hope. She is so beautiful, her dark skin seems to glow. She has those big, dark, almond eyes that compliment her long, thick, black hair."

"When did you first meet her?" asked Dr. Sunn.

"Oh, here we go again," said Snow. "It almost hurts to go back into my memories, so many of them are blocked, and I can get a horrible headache if I push. But when it comes to certain people, I can remember things, so I will give it a try. There was something I think when I was about eight or nine-years-old. My father always picked me up from school, except on Wednesdays when my Aunt Joy used to pick me up, but then Aunt Joy's son, Omar, started a study with other boys at the Mosque. So on Wednesday, I was able to walk home, and I loved that time alone. I felt strong, free, and like other kids when I walked home from school. One day, I got out early. The school had just started early dismissals from school on Wednesdays that day. I left school and was walking as fast as I could to get home. I didn't want my father to get mad at me."

"Snow, what was it that you were afraid of?" asked Dr. Sunn.

"Well, Dr. Sunn, I had to account for my every moment with my father. I know that bothered me, but I don't really know what I feared. I knew I had to hurry home and tell him I had gotten out of school early. I remember there was a girl in my class, and she had told me about a house she went to on Wednesdays after school. She said that there was a Bible Study at this house. I saw that girl that day while I was walking fast, trying to get home. She ran up to me, and she asked me why I was walking so fast. I told her that I could not talk to her or stop because if my father saw me stopping and talking to anyone, he would not let me walk home on Wednesdays anymore. I remember her saying to me, 'well, Snow, does your father know you got out early today?' No, I told her."

"Then come with me!" she said. "They are doing the Bible Study now. They want the kids to come. They said most of the kids will be alone on Wednesdays because of the early dismissal, so come on with me, we will have fun there, you'll see!"

Snow continued, "She acted so excited as she said, 'they have a cloth board there, and they tell Bible stories by putting cloth figures of people and other things on the board. They also give you snacks, maybe a little cake and punch to drink. Come on.' So, I went with her, and that was the first time I saw Hope. I walked in the door and there she was, standing like she was there waiting for me. She welcomed me with her beautiful smile. She gave me a strong hug and showed me a chair, asking me to sit next to her."

Snow went on, "Then I saw another woman there. She was using a felt board to tell the story of Moses. She was a nice lady, too, and she always smiled at all of us kids. I found hope that day because of the story about Moses. I thought if Moses was put in the water to die and he grew up to be a king and a prophet, that there was hope for me, too. So, I went there every Wednesday after school. I learned a lot about the bible. I even won a chocolate rabbit because of scriptures I had memorized. They were always so nice to me there. They gave me hugs and snacks to eat. I loved it, and my new friend Hope was always there."

"That's an amazing story, Snow," Dr. Sunn told her. "So, you have known Hope for a very long time? What about Aunty Kay and Louie?"

"Well, Dr. Sunn, I have always known Aunty Kay as long as I can remember. She was at my house when I was very little. She was there if I started to cry. She always came to me when I was lonely and wanted my mother. I can remember the first time I saw her, I was scared and lonely and crying for my mother, but she wasn't there, I couldn't find my mother anywhere. And then there was Aunty Kay. And really, Dr. Sunn, I do not know how a little Japanese woman came to live with me. When I think about it, I am going to ask her that one day."

"So, Snow, how did you meet Louie?" he said, changing the topic.

Louie, he is so tall and strong. The first time I saw Louie was the day my father found out that I had been leaving school early on Wednesdays. I had just gotten home, and I was so proud of myself and happy with my winnings. I was eating the chocolate rabbit. My father was standing out in front of the house. He was getting ready to get into his truck to come and get me. I can remember his face being red, and his blood vessels were sticking up. I could see them all puffy on his neck and on his face. They almost looked blue. That was the first time I was really scared of him."

"He started yelling at me, 'Snow, the school called and told me that there have been early dismissals on Wednesdays!' He demanded that I tell him where I had been. He screamed at me, 'Where the hell have you been going to for the last three months?'"

"So, I told him. I told him everything. I told him about Hope and the Bible Study. He hit the chocolate rabbit out of my hands. Then he grabbed me up, and just as he did at that precise instant, Louie was there. He yelled at my father, 'Put her down!' My father was stunned. Then Louie began to hit my father, and my father began to hit and kick Louie. I passed out. Later, I woke up in my bed. Aunty Kay was there. She told me I could not go back to the Bible Study. She told me to stay away from Hope. She said, 'Snow, there is no hope, not here, just obedience to the father.' She said, 'Stop crying, Snow, from now on, whenever someone tries to hurt you, I'll call Louie, and he will protect you.' She wiped my forehead and gave me a kiss. I must have passed out again. I was sick for two weeks. I remember that I hurt all over and just stayed in bed. My father only gave me soup to eat. One night before I went back to school, my father told me that the school had called him. He said that I could go back to school. Then he made me promise that I would not go back to the Bible Study or talk to anyone on my way home. He made me swear on my mom. That night, Aunty Kay was there. She told me if I didn't do what my father said, my mother would die. I was scared of that threat. It really shook me, so I never went back to the Bible study."

"That's a sad story, Snow," he told her. "Things like that should never happen to little girls."

"That's okay, Dr. Sunn. You know that when I would walk past the house with the Bible Study, Hope would be waiting. Hope would be on the front steps, or she would be looking out of the window. When she would see me, she would come out to meet me and she would walk me home, she would say good-bye when we reached my block. She would smile at me and tell me to always keep hope and me in your heart, and that one day, things would be okay. She did this for the rest of the school year. She was like that mail slogan, 'neither rain, snow, sleet, nor dead of night,' she was there for me. After that, sometimes I would see her at a distance, at a store, or in a park or just walking down the street."

Dr. Sunn put his pad down and looked up at Snow. "You're making progress with your memories and overall in your therapy, too. I was hesitant, but I believe we are ready to stroke your subconscious a little more. Dr. Sunn bent down and opened up his desk drawer. He reached in and pulled out the blue coat. He slowly handed it to Snow.

Chapter Seven

Revelations

Snow grabbed the coat and pulled it towards herself. She buried her nose into the soft white fur. As she took a deep breath in, her memories ignited, triggering one after another. She heard her mother's voice, 'I'll always love you, stay strong.' Instantly, she was back on the floor with her mother.

"Look, Snow," she said. "If we pull back the carpet, there's a hole here where this pipe runs down the radiator. We can see into the kitchen from here." The light shone up from the kitchen. Snow's mother put her finger in front of her lip, shhhh, she whispered. "Keep your voice low, so he won't hear us."

Snow watched her mother adjust her long hair as she moved closer to the hole in the floor, so she could look down. She motioned for Snow to move closer. They both sat there, watching her father move around in the kitchen. Snow looked at her mother's face, she was beautiful, she did not look insane. With a jerk, Snow was brought back from the past into the present moment.

Snow sat there, fully shaken by the strong memory. She had remembered her mother's breath, her smell, and her long, flowing blonde hair. Snow thought to herself, steady, girl. Get up slowly, do not alarm

Dr. Sunn. She told herself, you need to be in group tonight to support Baby Girl and Dawn and to confront Aunty Kay.

She heard Dr. Sunn's voice. "Are you okay, Snow?" he asked as he looked into her eyes.

"Yes, I'm good," she said. "I just had a flood of old memories, that's good, right?"

"Yes, of course," replied Dr. Sunn.

"I need to go now. Can I take the coat?" she asked.

"Yes, yes, it's yours," he told her.

Snow left the office, clutching her old blue coat to her body. Dr. Sunn finished his notes and his report on Snow for Dr. Rose.

Louie found Aunty Kay sitting outside in the garden area.

She heard Louie walk up. It's just so beautiful out here, she thought to herself. The weather is getting warmer, I can feel the sun on my face and hear the birds sing, I'll never give this up. It's just a perfect day.

"Aunty Kay," said Louie in a quivering voice. "We might have a problem."

Aunty Kay turned her head to look at Louie.

He continued, "I've kind of locked Baby Girl and Dawn both up together in the safe room."

"What have you done, Louie? We need to go now, right now!" Aunty Kay said in a firm voice. "Let's go, now!"

"Uh, how about the group?" he asked her. "What's going to happen if we do not show?"

"Okay, you're right. I will just have to straighten out this mess you made later after group. Let's go, first to the group, then to the safe room," she decided.

• • • • •

Dr. Sunn walked up the squeaking metal stairs leading to the group room. He took a deep breath and walked through the door. He immediately noticed that there were only five chairs in the circle, peculiar, he thought.

Snow looked up at him and smiled. "Let's wait a few minutes for Baby Girl and Dawn. I've called them, but they haven't answered me. Has anyone else seen either one of them?"

"Well," said Dr. Sunn, "Dawn missed her session, which I thought was very strange."

Louie spoke up, "No, we haven't heard from either one of them either."

"Interesting," said Dr. Sunn. "By the way, who set up the group room for group tonight?"

"Ah, that would be me," said Louie.

"Well, Louie, why are there only five chairs?" Dr. Sunn questioned. "You must have known there would only be five in group tonight."

"That's right!" added Snow, "where are they, and how did you know they weren't coming, Louie?"

"Let's just cancel group if they are not coming. Let's just go," said Aunty Kay.

"No," interjected Hope. "Let's start group without them."

"Really," said Aunty Kay. "Whatever the group leader wants to do, I'm okay with that."

"Good," said Snow. "We all then agree to start. Let me start. I want to start this group session by saying we need some boundaries," Snow said as she smiled at Dr. Sunn. "What happened in the last group cannot happen again. We need to stay in the moment and focus, so we can process the events, feelings, and thoughts that are driving our behaviors."

"Snow, what boundaries do you feel we need?" asked Aunty Kay.

"Well, we need to be respectful, kind and considerate of each other's feelings and thoughts, and no physical aggression at all," she answered.

"I'm sorry," said Louie.

"So am I," replied Aunty Kay.

"Well, good then. Let's start with talking about our mothers." Snow went on. "I had a memory about my mother today. It was amazing. I saw her face, her hair, and I could feel her breath."

Aunty Kay, panicking, quickly interrupted. "Is that so, Louie, he had a memory, too. Isn't that right, Louie? You had a touching memory about your mother, too. Go on, tell them Louie."

"I'm-m-m not sure what you are talking about," said Louie, stammering for words.

"Louie, remember you told me about a memory you had?" she asked. "It was about your father when he was sitting on your mother and she was on the floor. He was holding her hands over her head, and he made you scratch her face with your nails until she was bleeding."

"What the hell," yelled Louie. "How did you know that? I never told you that, I have never told anyone that!"

Dr. Sunn tensed up, he could fill the energy in the room go from positive to negative, as he watched the pictures of Louie and Aunty Kay fall to the floor from Snow's hands.

There was a scream. "SHUT UP!" But Snow did not know who was screaming or where it came from or who was yelling. Then there was a strange feeling that began to move up from Snow's inner stomach. The feeling engulfed her, it was paralyzing her. She saw her mother on the floor. She heard her father yelling and swearing at her.

"Scratch her, scratch her face, you little bitch," her father was yelling. She could see Louie on top of her mother. The next thing she saw was the floor giving way. It began to break into pieces. She saw blue carpet, and she was heading straight for it. The carpet just tore apart as she fell into it. She broke through the floor in her mother's room, falling. She was headed toward the old kitchen floor now, still falling hard and fast in the house she had grew up in. Franticly, she tried to make sense of things. So dizzy! How could she magically be transported back through time to her old house? Everything around her; furniture, vases, table lamps, all started to crash and break apart as she fell through the floor. Time slowed down, seconds became minutes, minutes became hours as she floated down, down. As she gently hit the kitchen floor, it gave away, too. She continued her fall all in slow motion.

Dr. Sunn stood above Snow. She laid motionless on the floor. He hit code orange on his pager, and within minutes, the night staff burst into the room. "Get her back to her room. Hurry!"

Aunty Kay barked an order out to Louie, "Let's go now, move." They ran as fast as they could down the corridors. They ran together toward the safe room. Once in front of the heavy locked door, Aunty Kay ordered Louie to open it quickly. Once inside, they slammed the door shut. Dawn was laying on a bed, twirling the thin veil with her fingers, and singing a Hank William's song, *I'm So Lonesome I Could Cry*. She turned to look at the commotion, then gave a shrug and turned toward the wall. Baby Girl was on the bed crying.

"Aunty Kay, help me!" Baby Girl said crying. "That mean Louie locked me in here. Where are my dolls, are they okay?"

"Louie, Louie, what have you done?" Aunty Kay questioned. "By locking Baby Girl up without her dolls, you robbed her of safety, happiness, and her sense of self. Our world is coming to an end. Can't you feel the shaking? The threat is real."

"Who cares," injected Dawn with her southern drawl.

Louie ignored Dawn and went on to question Aunty Kay, "Why did you tell the group about Martha and that I had scratched her face? Now everyone knows, including Dr. Sunn."

"Louie, I tried to stop Snow," she replied. "She is getting too strong. This world, our world, is safe for her. We have all been safe in a delusional world, one with repressed memories and thoughts."

"Aunty Kay, what are you saying?" Asked Louie. "And what happened in there? What is happening now, and how did you know what happened with the father and me?"

"Louie, really, don't you understand I know everything?" she told him. "I know everything about you and Snow and everyone in the group. I'm the leader. I have control over everyone, and orders have to come from me! But you broke command by using the safe room without my consent. You polluted our world, and it is now toxic."

"Told you so," yelled Dawn from her bed.

"Listen to me, everyone, I can fix this. You all just stay here," Aunty Kay ordered.

"No!" yelled everyone in one collective voice. But just then, Snow came crashing through the ceiling.

Dr. Sunn was sitting in Snow's room. He had just given her an injection.

"Wake up, Snow," he said as he put a cool cloth on her face. But Snow was not there. She was falling through time in her world, a world that only existed in her mind. Dr. Sunn sat staring down at Snow, looking for any movement. Just then, she opened her eyes.

"Snow, you opened your eyes. Are you ok now?" Dr. Sunn asked as he observed her.

"No, I'm not Snow. It's me, Hope."

Dr. Sunn looked more closely. Yes, it was indeed Hope. She always presented herself with that recognizable smile and aura of peacefulness. Dr. Sunn had come to know them all. Each with their own unique facial expressions, mannerisms, speech, and personality.

"Can you get Snow for me Hope?" asked Dr. Sunn.

"No, she won't answer," she told him.

"I've searched, but I can't find her. Hope, what is going on?" asked Dr. Sunn.

"Well, I believe that Aunty Kay has done something," she explained. "I'm not sure what yet, but I'm going to find out, and I will find Aunty Kay, even though she won't answer. No one is responding to me. I must go and investigate this. I need to talk to another alter, so I will understand what is going on."

"Okay but be careful, Hope," he told her.

"I'm strong, Dr. Sunn," she assured him. "I'm different. I'm not just from the subconscious, my origin is from the soul, and I have a spark of the Spirit!"

"Oh, I see," said Dr. Sunn in a slightly condescending voice. "How interesting, but please, be careful. I don't want to lose communications with you or Snow."

"Dr. Sunn, if for some reason I disappear like Bud did, you'll see me in a wish, a belief, or in her faith. Dr. Sunn, you know better than any of us that Snow can only truly survive if we merge. One more thing, find the blue coat. Inside the lining there is a letter from the Mother. I have to find that control freak Aunty Kay!" Then Hope's eyes rolled back into her head. Snow's body became limp and non-responsive.

Hope walked through the dark passageway searching for Aunty Kay and Louie. She looked in Aunty Kay's room first, then in Louie's, but there was just emptiness. Maybe I'll get lucky in Baby Girl's room, she thought. Of course, Aunty Kay must be threatening them with something hideous. Well, get ready, Aunty Kay, here comes Hope! Hope burst into Baby Girl's room, expecting a fight. "No one is here either," she thought out loud. Then she saw the dolls. "Wow, something is wrong here. Baby Girl would never go off for any length of time without her dolls. I'll find them," she said out loud as she walked out into the darkness through the corridor, carrying the dolls.

"What the heck, where am I?" said Snow. "This looks like the tornado room in my old house, the house that I grew up in."

"You're here with us," said Baby Girl. Then she whispered, "Nobody is safe."

Snow looked around the room, and memories came rushing in.

Aunty Kay moved in closer to Snow and then said, "Everyone just be quiet, no one say another word. Snow, you need to trust me. I have tried to protect you, Snow, and protect all of us. Things were going good but then that crazy Southern whore had to talk about the mother, and Baby Girl told on the father. Well, I have always said that the truth will kill. So, now we are going to have group, a real group, and as it always has been and as it should be, I am the leader! I hope we can survive. This world, our world, is made up of shadows and glimpses. We can only hope to see our existence in this fragile world. We are mere representatives of thoughts. And if we can only hope to know ourselves, how can we know anything. So, let's start, but remember, we are all on shaky ground."

Turning toward Snow, Aunty Kay said, "So, you can remember the safe room, well, Snow, do you know why it's called the safe room?"

"Yes," answered Snow, "it was made to keep us safe when there were tornadoes."

"True," said Aunty Kay, "initially that is why the builders built it to the father's specifications. The father called it his safe room. And that's because he would lock the mother and sometimes you in here, so he would be safe. The father put a lot of foresight into designing this room, the corridors, and escape doors."

"What are you talking about? That does not make sense. Why would my father not be safe, and are you saying he was frightened? Of what?"

"Well, you and the mother both attacked him," she replied. "The mother hated him, and you hate him. You both have hurt him!"

"I never tried to hurt my father!" said Snow.

"Oh, really," said Aunty Kay. "You don't remember attacking your father?"

"No, I never did," she denied. "What is she talking about, does anyone know?"

"She is just twisting things again," said Dawn.

"Oh, really, lets unravel the truth and bring light to the shadow," Aunty Kay went on to say in an accusing tone. "It wasn't Louie that fought the father the day you were disobedient in the front yard, it was you, Snow. You lost control, you attacked the father, you screamed at the father, hitting him and kicking him."

"No, that was Louie!" she denied. "I have always respected my father, and I am too weak to do that anyway."

"No, Snow, it was you," replied Aunty Kay with a smirk.

Snow felt a sick feeling rising up into her throat.

"Snow, the Father built his safe room to protect him from the outsiders, the infidels," Aunty Kay went on to explain. "He knew the mother would try to bring the outsiders into his home. He also feared that you would bring the very people that hated him, people that would imprison him and take you and the mother away. This room was designed to keep everyone safe from all outside influences and storms. And I was fashioned to keep you safe, and so, I had to defend the image of the father."

Snow saw that the slanted window was opening. She heard Hope's voice as she called into the room.

"Snow, please come out here, I need to speak with you," pleaded Hope.

Aunty Kay went to the window and spoke, "Hope, you were not asked to join this group. Go away."

"I am only here to help," she continued. "Look, I have One, Two, and Three with me."

Hearing that, Baby Girl began to bellow out, "My dolls, my dolls!"

Aunty Kay tried to quiet her, but Baby Girl just became louder and louder.

"Okay, we will let Hope come in and bring the dolls, but remember, we must proceed carefully."

Aunty Kay went to the door and unlocked it with her key, and Hope stepped in.

Hope walked over to Baby Girl and gently handed her her dolls. Smiling, she said, "We are, number One, now safe, Two is now happy again, and Three, you are agreeable."

"Good," said Hope. "Now, let's get Aunty Kay." They all rushed toward Aunty Kay, knocking her off her feet. Louie held her down even as she started shouting out demands.

Everyone called to Snow to take back control of the group.

"Stop it, stop it!" yelled Snow as she pushed Louie off and then helped Aunty Kay get back up.

"Really," said Aunty Kay. "I think you all need to continue to be safe. I'm tired of trying to keep everyone safe and alive. This has been hard for me, too. I'm done. All of you will remain in this place. I choose to emerge and control." Aunty Kay ran toward the door. Hope reached out to grab her, but it was too late. Aunty Kay was out of the safe room. She slammed the door shut and then locked it.

Snow stood at the door, pounding on it, screaming, "Let me out, let me out." Hope walked over to her and comforted her by putting her arms around her and giving her a big hug.

"Snow," said Hope, "we must talk. Come over here and sit down next to me." Hope led Snow away from the door to a couch. Aunty Kay was right about unveiling the truth, but it will not kill you, and I believe it will set you free."

Dawn interrupted, "Aunty Kay is so full of hate. She has always been mean and hateful."

"That's not completely true. She only wants to protect Snow," said Hope as she smiled up at Snow while taking her hand in hers. "Think about it. She struggles to keep a positive image of your father. Ask yourself, why?"

"What are you saying? This is nonsense. I don't know what to think," Snow said. "You might be right about her protecting my father because she even accused me of attacking him. Like I would attack a man as big and powerful as my father?"

"We can talk about that later, but for now, let's focus on Aunty Kay," Hope went on. "Snow, she fears your father. She is afraid if you saw the truth about him, it would have destroyed you, so she guarded against it. She also knows that your father created an illusion, where he lived as the strong protective father. His delusional world could not be questioned by you. He needed you to believe and live out the lie with him.

The father kidnapped your mother, held her captive, drugged her routinely, and made you think she was insane. He had to live here in the states until he completed his assignment for a vast Islamic network he was involved with. He was trapped here. His plan was ultimately to escape back to Iran."

"What are you talking about, Hope? asked Snow. "I'm so confused by all of this."

"First, you need to know we all love you, and we are going to help you through this. Doesn't it seem strange that you knew us all in your childhood and that Aunty Kay has always been with you. She first emerged to protect you from seeing the truth about your father. Snow, she is a powerful source in your sub conscious. She has fought to keep you sane through a horrendous and unspeakable childhood."

Snow began to laugh, "She kept me sane? Well, I feel pretty insane right now! I'm locked up in a room I remember from my childhood home, I was unresponsive for a year in the state hospital, is that sane?"

"Snow, you grew up in a home so hideous that Aunty Kay caused you to fragment," said Hope.

"What are you saying?" asked Snow.

"Louie, get over here," yelled Hope.

"No, I'm not feeling good about this," he replied.

"Louie, it is time, now talk to Snow," Hope said as she pushed Louie toward Snow.

"It's true, Snow," explained Louie. "Aunty Kay called me out when your father started to beat you in the front yard, just like she said. You had already seen and dealt with things that a little girl should never have to see, even in a fiction movie, but it was real, it was your daily life. You lived with it and through it. I was there to take the punches and the kicks. I stood between you and the hateful words, all of it landed on me, not on you. And after that, whenever you needed to fight or when your father became aggressive, I took over. Snow, think about it.

Why are your memories in so many tiny pieces? They break off and then start up again days, weeks, and even months later?"

"Wow!" said the shaken Snow. "And what about you, Dawn?"

"Honey, you know I love you," said Dawn. "What I'm going to say is bizarre, but factual! Aunty Kay called me out to protect you from what you saw the father do to the mother." Snow gasps for her breath as images of abuse ran across her mind. "Snow, I have daddy issues, so you wouldn't. I was the one that witnessed the mother being tortured and sexually abused by the father. Snow, as we disappear just as Bud did, you will remember all of this for yourself."

"What about Bud?" Snow asked.

"Snow," Hope replied, "Bud showed up when you needed a friend, right?"

"Okay, now explain, Baby Girl," Snow questioned.

"It wasn't Baby Girl sexually abused and given as a child bride, it was you, Snow."

"I can't believe that," sobbed Snow. How could I not be aware of that, remember it, or feel it."

Hope explained, "Honey, because Aunty Kay called out Baby Girl, and she suffered that ungodly abuse, so you would not remember it. Snow, we are just fragments of you."

"Then who in the hell is Aunty Kay? Tell me that, anyone of you or should I tell myself?"

"Honey, she is you!" Hope told her.

"If I believe what you are saying, I am talking to myself." Snow began to laugh at the thought that she was not having a conversation with four other people but was holding the conversation alone with herself. Snow watched in amazement as the room began to turn white with a florescent glow. The room shone bright and became brighter and brighter until the walls were gone, there was no one else but her. Hope, Louie, Dawn, and Baby Girl all had disappeared, evaporated like a foggy mist in the sun. She watched as a big, fluffy snowflake fell gently down on her face. She laughed and then fell face first into the white, beautiful, comforting snow. There was nothing else, no pain, no anger, no sadness, just the beautiful white snow. Snow went into a second catatonic state.

Chapter Eight

The Letter

Dr. Sunn picked up the blue coat that was lying on the chair just as Snow had left it. He examined the coat, turning it upside down. He put his hand on the soft silver lining. As he ran his hand down the cloth, he felt something. He saw that the thread was of a different color. He pulled out his pocket knife and cut the thread. He reached into the inside of the lining and pulled out a letter. He unfolded the letter and saw it was written in crayon, he began to read:

> Hello, my name is Martha DuTro. I have been missing for 14 years. I was 13 when I first Met Ali, I was 14 when my daughter, Snow, was born. The day I met Ali was a cold day in more than just one way. I had just gotten off of my school bus and was walking home. I had said good bye to my friends and then I slipped on the ice, falling and hitting my head on the ice. As I looked up, I saw what I thought was an angel standing above me. He had a gray aura though, another warning I ignored. He had fluffy, curly brown hair and big green eyes. He reached down and extended his smooth,

brown hand to me, so I took it, and he pulled me up. He helped me brush off the snow, and we both laughed. He told me he was a pharmacist and that he worked across the street at the drug store. After our first meeting, he would regularly wait for me and walk with me to my block. I felt special that such a handsome man and an older man of 25 would take such an interest in me. I knew I should tell someone, but I did not want to lose what I was feeling. After all, I told myself, what was wrong with me allowing him to walk with me home. He asked a lot of questions, and he gave me a lot of attention and compliments. He said he loved my singing, and he would applaud me when I danced, just as my brother Kenneth had done. I'm not making excuses for myself, but I still was grieving Kenneth's death, and I missed him. Ali helped to fill that empty place in my heart. Did I know better? Yes, I had been warned.

One day, Ali invited me to walk across the street to get a cup of hot chocolate. Again, I thought no harm. We walked across the street toward the restaurant. We were almost ready to walk in the door when he told me he had left his wallet in his car. So, I walked with him. I did not notice any red flags or any alarms. Ali was my friend, he was so handsome and what a smile he had! I wish someone could have told me that the boogeyman was not ugly. Once we reached his car, he opened the door and pulled out a rag, I still remember the smell as he covered my nose and mouth with the soaked rag. I woke up hours later. It was dark, I didn't know where I was, and I was chained to a bed. Ali and his brother, Badeel, stood at the foot of the bed. Badeel only said, "You are to be my brother's wife. Any attempt to escape will be deadly. You will be cut down instantly without hesitation, so don't even try it."

I'm writing this in hope that whoever finds this letter will intervene and not send Snow back here to her father, Ali. I am Snow's mother, and if you are reading this letter, I am still his prisoner or dead. Ali, my capturer, has kept me a prisoner here under the threat of death. I am perfectly sane most of the time. He drugs me, and during those times, I feel insane. He has convinced Snow that I am crazy. He drugs me whenever anyone from the outside must come here. He also built a safe room under the stairs. He often locks me in there for weeks. If you can't find me during the rescue attempt, check the room under the stairs. You can find me at 825 Westmoreland Pl. I cannot give more details since I am under a time constraint. He might catch me at any time writing this. He has also threatened to kill Snow if I try to escape. That is why I am writing this and hiding it in her coat. I know she is safe. If someone is reading this, please contact the local authorities. My parents' names are Jack and Anna DuTro, they will verify my disappearance.

Today is Valentine's day. I am sending Snow out with this letter. Please hurry.

Chapter Nine

Planning a Valentine's Day Surprise

About three years earlier, Martha woke up with a feeling of resolve. Martha started rethinking her life as a captive, and her mind wandered back to past events.

She had lived under a death threat since she first woke up chained to a bed. Ali was her capturer, and Badeel was her consequence. She had survived unspeakable abuse and torture as Ali's wife, concubine, really just his sex slave, she thought to herself. Going over everything in her mind, I was right in keeping my pregnancy hidden from him until I was able to deliver my baby. Maybe I was selfish by birthing Snow, but I had to. I needed her to survive, just to have someone who would love me. Well, she thought, that did not work out like I thought. I was wrong, but I loved Snow from that first moment I saw her. I'm so glad and I thank GOD that I had my baby. I had to protect life, even though Ali is a devil and she was born into this hellish nightmare. She is so innocent, and she was such a beautiful baby. Her olive color skin was so soft. She has those large green eyes with thick black lashes. The wispy brown curls that framed her face were so beautiful and so perfect. Yes, even though I was drugged with all kinds of cocktails, shot up by Ali sometimes daily and with all the drugs he used, some hallucinogens, uppers, downers, maybe even horse sedatives. But Snow is good and not affected by the drugs. She is perfect, and she is so smart, I thank you, GOD. Yes, I was able to keep my pregnancy hidden and deceive Ali. It was a cold-snowy night when I had her. I was in so much pain, but I gave birth in silence. It was two weeks before Ali saw the baby. And thank you, GOD, for the two-month trip that took Ali back to his home in Iran. It was those two months that gave me the needed time to successfully conceal my pregnancy from him.

He waited at least a week before going into my room. The day he met Snow, he came in the room, drunk as usual, on fire with his perverted sexual cravings. He approached the bed calling me a bitch, telling me what he was going to do to me. He ripped the covers off and pulled me out of the bed by my hair. That's when the baby cried out. When he heard the cry, he was so startled, he fell back, leaving me go. I jumped back into the bed and cradled the baby, trying to hide her from his evil sight. Promising her in a whisper, I will always protect you. Then Ali's loud drunken voice rang out, "What the hell is going on here, bitch? Where did you get that thing from?" I can remember the feeling of power that came over me. I was able to yell back, "She is a baby, your baby and my baby!" Thinking back to that night, she remembered the promise she had made to Ali, "I promise as long as you let Snow stay here with me and live, I will not try to run away again."

Martha was true to her promise. She sometimes thought that he came to love Snow, 'the Better Ali' usually was there when Snow was involved. He did let her stay after all, in many ways she was like other kids. Martha thought back to playing and singing London Bridge is falling. She did try to make life as close to a normal childhood as she could for Snow.

But then, that evil man, Ali, gave Snow to Badeel as a child bride when she was only nine. That night was the worst night of my life, she thought. I could not protect my daughter from that pig, those cruel, hateful, evil men. Martha put the crippling thought away, she had learned how to control her thoughts in order to survive. Yes, even after that night, she stayed strong for Snow and herself. With help from Badeel's first wife, Joy, she was able to persuade Ali that Snow needed to stay at the house and in the states. After all, Snow did not have the skills or knowledge to survive as a wife in Iran. Ali agreed that Snow could continue to stay and live in the house until Badeel came for her. And now that Snow turned 13, he wanted her in Iran.

The day Martha knew she would no longer keep her promise about running away was the day she was watching Ali through the register hole in her floor. She heard voices, it was Ali and Joy. That was a week before Valentine's Day, she was 27.

They were talking about Snow and Badeel. She heard Ali and Joy making plans. She heard Joy telling Ali that she had started the passport process for herself, her son, and Snow. She heard how enthusiastic Joy was about going to Iran with her son, being the number one wife in Badeel's house. She did not seem to be at all bothered when she discussed the plan to take Snow. She only seemed to want Ali and Badeel's approval. Martha felt sick when she heard the excitement in Joy's voice as she told Ali, "I know how men are, and Badeel will be so happy with me for bringing him his young, beautiful wife." Martha knew at that second that if she was going to save Snow, she would need a plan of her own.

At first, Martha felt hopeless and discouraged. She started to look around her room, her mind franticly searching and reaching for an idea, any idea. There had to be something in here, she thought. Looking around her room, she took a hasty inventory. The room was filled with books, some crayons, and paper. She had CDs and a CD player. What am I thinking, what can I do, I am a prisoner, a captive for a man that holds disdain for all womanhood. I have not even been allowed to watch TV for 14 years. No one ever sees me, I can only look out of this protected window and see the back yard. The film keeps anyone from seeing in. I have no help. No one other than Ali, Badeel, Joy, and Ali's so-called Doctor had seen me. He probably is some kind of veterinarian. Then there is Snow, my daughter, who was taught that I am deranged, and yes, I did allow her to believe that. Again, I guarded Snow's safety by allowing her not to see the truth. As long as she believed Ali was not the monster he is, she has been safe and sheltered.

But now is the time to unveil the truth, she thought. I must do something. Snow had witnessed many incidents of cruelty, and after Badeel brutally forced himself on her, my little nine-year-old Snow, Martha again began to cry just remembering that day. She went on to think that that was when I had first sensed a change in Snow. I witnessed how an evil act changed my little girl, and how could Snow not been changed after her innocence was taken from her.

I did try to help her heal, I gave her the dolls she named One, Two, and Three. I was able to help Snow by giving her those dolls that Ali had given me when I was first imprisoned here. Martha smiled as she remembered the night Snow was allowed to visit her in her room. She thought back to the day when Snow had named them. She could almost hear Snow saying, "One, you are safe, Two, you are happy, and Three, you are sweet." She thought how Ali stood there watching as I tried to give comfort to my poor little Snow. What an evil bastard. His own daughter given up as a child bride, and now his plan was to send her to Iran to live forever with that selfish, brutal, nasty criminal.

"Focus," Martha said aloud to herself. "What can I do now?" Martha opened her closet and there was the answer, her beautiful blue coat. The one she was wearing the day she was taken. Thoughts of her past came flooding back. She was thinking about the day her mother had bought her the coat. It was so beautiful, and it was stylish.

She could hear her own mother say, "This is a young woman's coat. You're getting older now, Martha, this is the type of coat a young woman like you should wear, and I'm going to buy it for you. A gift from a mother to her daughter to mark the passage of becoming a teenager."

SNOW AT THE DOME

Martha remembered how beautiful and proud she felt that day. Again, stay focused, she thought out loud. She sat down and grabbed her needle and thread. Ali did not allow her to have anything sharp. Scissors would be good right now, she thought. She ripped the thread from an inside seam. She took out one of the crayons from her bin and some paper. She quickly wrote a short letter, folding it and creasing it tightly, she stuck it in between the lining. She skillfully stitched the hem back. Then she found a small patch of cloth and embroidered, "Snow DuTro" on it. And then she sewed the cloth on the inside of the coat.

She would have to talk to that moose of a woman, Joy. And, of course, she would have to flatter her and then suggest that Snow should have her coat, a mother's gift to a daughter. The plan started to evolve. Martha followed through with her talk to Joy about the coat. Yes, just one look at the coat and Joy agreed. "I know this coat, it's a Toscana, and it is the one that is hooded with the soft white fur. It's very valuable, and you don't have much to pass down to your daughter, Snow," Joy said as she ran her fingers on the coat.

Quickly, Martha grabbed the coat to herself and said, "If Ali agrees, I want to give it to Snow myself."

"It is written that you will give Snow this coat," Joy said as she walked out the door and closed it behind her.

Martha heard the familiar locking sound and that sound generated a new part of the plan.

Later that day, she heard the door unlock and in walked Joy, followed by Snow. Joy said, "Good news. Ali has agreed to let you give Snow the coat after I suggested it to him. He also wants to start you back on your 5pm medication. Please let me give it to you quickly, and please, without a fuss. After all, I have supported you, yes?"

"Yes, you have, Joy, but just let me talk with Snow before?" Martha asked.

"No," replied Joy, "I must get home to my son, now hurry up."

Martha extended her arm. Then she turned around and gave Snow the coat. She was able to tell Snow that the coat had been hers and that her mother had given it to her when she was about the same age. She saw Snow look down and take the coat and then the medication hit her, and she began to talk nonsense. She needed to find her bed to lie down before she collapsed.

She remembered how she had to fight off the effects of the medication when Ali came in her room that night. She also remembered it, the better Ali, that night. Sometimes Martha thought there might be two of him: the better Ali, and the Evil Ali. Martha acted affectionate, which sickened her to her very core, and she concealed it well that night. Anyway, she was glad for another factor on her side. Martha was determined to get a promise from him to see Snow. "Ali, please let me see Snow, I just want to ask her about the coat. I want to know if she really likes it and finds it fashionable. Just a few minutes is all I ask. I will pleasure you tonight anyway you want, all I ask in exchange is to see my daughter for a few minutes."

Ali was taken aback. He just whispered the question, "When?"

"Tomorrow morning." Martha giggled as she remembered that silent victory.

The next morning when Snow came into Martha's room, she saw a smile on Snow's face. It was that smile that brought her hope and moved her into action.

"Snow," Martha asked, "will you take this note to school and ask your counselor, Mr. Graham, to come here to talk with your father on the 14th after school?"

Snow took the note from her mother and read it. Snow agreed.

Martha then added, "Please stay home for Valentine's day." As Snow walked away, a feeling of hope rose up from Martha's stomach, and she gasped out a sigh of relief.

Chapter Ten

Time to Go

Martha's D-day. Knowing that this was the day she would put her life and Snow's on the line. She had everything in place. Her plans would soon go into action. Once started, she would just have to let it run its course. She knew once the doorbell rang, it was a go. She felt a strange tingling run through her body.

Martha's thoughts brought her to this day. It was the 14th, Valentine's day. The security gate would soon buzz. Ali would look through the monitor and see an infidel at the gate. Ali will follow through as he always did when surprised by some outsider coming to the house. His need for absolute power to protect his charade. He would order her to the safe room, along with Snow. If he wants to prove that I'm insane, he will shoot me up, she thought. Either way, he will have an injection ready, just in case he feels he needs to use it. Martha hoped that Mr. Graham would ring the bell before 5pm. Ali routinely gave her an injection around that time.

Martha heard the security gate alarm. She rolled up a piece of the cardboard from the empty toilet tissue roll and stuck it in her bra.

Instantly, Ali was at the door to the safe room. "Now," he ordered. Next, he stopped at Snow's door and yelled out his order, "Safe room, now." Ali hushed, then as he ushered them to the safe room. Once at the door, Martha swiftly took the carboard from her bra and jammed it into the latch. Once in the room, Ali pulled a syringe out, saying, "Extend your arm. Hurry, now!"

Martha backed up pleading, "No, no, please!" She could hear the man's voice of the intercom identifying himself as Mr. Graham.

"I'll be back," said Ali as he quickly laid the syringe down on the counter top. Ali then turned and rushed through the door, slamming it behind him.

Snow stood with her mouth open, staring at Martha. "Mother, father is going to be mad at you."

"Stop it now, Snow, and listen to me. That stuff in the syringe is not medicine, it's drugs. Ali, your father shoots me up with them. I've been a prisoner since I was 13, your age. Your father is involved with an Iranian sleeper cell, and they hate Americans and our way of life. He plans on taking you to Iran. Think about it. You must remember things you saw. How no one is allowed over, you can't even have a friend."

"No, Mother," Snow told her. "I do have friends. Bud and Hope are my friends. They come here a lot."

Martha was confused by Snow's response, but she just kept pushing on, knowing that this may be her only opportunity to convince Snow to run with her.

"Snow, Ali is planning on sending you to Iran to live with Badeel to be one of his wives," her mother tried to explain.

"That cannot be true, Mother," she denied. "You are having trouble thinking because Father was not able to give you your medicine."

"No," Martha replied anxiously, trying to make her point. "Don't you remember what your father allowed Badeel to do to you?"

Snow looked intensely at her Mother, thinking about her reply. "You are really sick, Mother, just calm yourself. Father will be back soon."

"Why can't you remember what has happened and what you have lived through yourself?" she asked pleadingly. "Listen, Snow, we only have a few minutes. You must trust me. Listen to me, please! I hope I can push this door open. You can wait here, I will call a cab to take us to a friend. Dr. Rose is the chief psychiatrist at the hospital, he's been a family friend since I can remember, he is my father's best friend and the only person we can trust. Ali has so many connections, so many people have been paid off, there's a huge network. We will be safe with Dr. Rose, but we first must get to him. I am going to try to push this door open and then run to get your coat. Then all we have to do is get into the cab. Once you're in the cab, give the driver this hundred-dollar bill. I might be busy fighting off your dad or something, so just hand it to him. You will save your life and maybe mine. Remember, if anything happens when you get there, just call out for Dr. Rose. If I am not with you, give him your coat." With that, Martha slammed her body into the door with all of her might, and it opened. Martha ran up the stairs, grabbing the coat. She then went to the kitchen to call a cab and gave them instructions to follow. She then erased all numbers and dialed 66.

Snow sat there in shock, not really knowing what to do. She was trembling, and her hands were shaking.

Just then, Hope walked into the safe room and told her, "Snow, you must trust your mother."

"My mother is paranoid!" Snow tried to reason.

"Snow, if you can't trust your mother, trust me," she told her.

"Come on, let's go now!" yelled Martha.

Snow stood up and darted out of the room with Martha.

Martha ran with Snow across the yard to the gate. It had been left open after Mr. Graham was allowed in. They ran about two blocks. That was when Martha saw the cab sitting just around the corner. Almost there, she thought. Then she felt something stopping her, it was Ali. He had her by the arm and was pulling her back. She began to struggle to get away from him. He had the syringe in his hand. He was yelling at Snow to stop and to come back as he was trying to stick Martha with the needle. Then Snow was there, and she was trying to help her mother. As they struggled, Ali tried to plunge the needle into Martha's arm again, but he missed, sticking the needle into Snow's hand.

"Run, run now to the cab," yelled Martha. Martha was hitting and struggling with Ali. She jumped on his back, hitting, punching, and pulling his hair. She could see Snow running. She ran and made it to the cab. Martha saw her as she climbed into the cab. The cab took off as Martha watched in a haze. She watched it as it drove away and became smaller and smaller, then disappeared. Martha's eyes were fixed at the distance. She did not see Ali's punch coming that hit her square in her face. She just fell backward into darkness.

The day they lost their daughter, Ali did not consider Martha's loss. He could only see from his fascist perception. He took his frustration and his perceived privilege as a husband out on Snow's mother.

Ali sat looking at Martha as she was chained to her bed with abhorrence. Ali was furious! Snow was gone, and Martha was responsible. How dare she exalt herself in opposition to defile him. Ali grabbed the whip, and he beat Martha. Her pleads and screams did not penetrate or move Ali. He thought to himself, at least I did not follow Badeel's advice, although this beating may result in it. After Ali was satisfied that he had taught his captive wife her lesson, he called Joy into Martha's room telling her, "Take care of her, Joy. If she dies, let me know immediately."

CHAPTER ELEVEN

MARTHA

Martha DuTro was born in 1955 to Jack and Anna DuTro. She was their second child born to them. The couple's first child, Kenneth, had been born in 1948. He died during a combat mission in Vietnam in 1968 at a place called Khe Sanh. The couple was devastated with the loss of their only son, and Martha was heartbroken. Kenny, as she called him, had been more than a brother. He was her best friend. He always encouraged her to go for her dreams. Kenny had been talented. He could play almost any stringed instrument and he wrote songs. Kenny and Martha practiced music together. They had their own act they called the 'Starlights.' They had played together in some of the local halls and were a favorite at the street dances. Because of their loss, Anna and Jack lavished even more of their love on Martha. The DuTro's were a Christian family. They taught Martha about the love of the Father, GOD. They explained that GOD had welcomed Kenneth home, and whatever purpose GOD had intended for their boy would be fulfilled in heaven by the Father. During Martha's captive years, she would need to remember her parent's faith to find her own.

When Martha was a child, it was easy to indulge her. She was captivating, and she loved to entertain everyone with her big bright smile, beautiful voice, piano playing, and her dancing. Anna would often tell her friends that she had her own little Shirley Temple in Martha. Before Kenny died, when anyone asked Martha what she wanted to be when she grew up, she would say, "An entertainer, of course. Kenny and I will make the Starlights a sensation. Kenny will write the music and play his guitar. I will play my piano and sing. We will be the number one act where ever we perform. We will be famous someday." After his death, Martha would just say, "I don't know, we lost our star when Kenny was killed."

She was an obedient child wanting to please both her mother and father. Her father adored her and spoiled her at all times. Her mother loved to spend time with her. They would do crafts and bake things like cookies and cakes. They loved to go shopping together, and they enjoyed each other's company daily. Martha had never reached the place in her teenage life where she did not want to spend time with her parents. She loved her parents, and Martha was loved by her parents, cousins, friends, teachers, and classmates.

After Martha's disappearance, her parents searched relentlessly for her. They appeared on all the television networks, offered thousands of dollars in rewards, put up photos, and worked close with the missing children's network. Her family and friends were all sick and broken hearted. Martha's parents and her friends diligently sought for her and followed every lead, which only led to more disappointments. Anna cried for days. After 72 hours had passed, she collapsed. Jack held back his tears until he was in his bed at night. He turned away toward the wall and silently cried. He would try to get his mind off it, but it would continue to scream in his head in silence, "Where is my little princess, and what could be happening to her right now?"

Their little girl Martha sat tied to a bed, realizing she had been kidnapped. She had been too trusting. She thought all men were honorable like her uncle and father. She felt safe in her home, school, town, and in her own country. The only thing she knew about Eastern Men and

Islam was what she had read in the Tales of Arabian Nights. She loved the stories and especially the story about Scheherazade and Shahrayar. She thought women's rights were about equal pay. Now she was in the hands of men who told her that she was lower than a dog, and she had no rights. Martha believed in her heart that she was a child of GOD. Martha's faith sustained her. She prayed every day, first for freedom and then for strength to keep her sanity for the moment, the day, and in the dark of night.

During the first few days of her capture, Ali presented her with gifts, three beautiful dolls, exotic rich foods, clothing, books, CDs, and jewelry. Ali was sure that he could win Martha's obedience and affection. He played by his rule book, which told him he could take a wife from his enemies, and she would be subject to him with no rights of her own. Martha begged to be set free and allowed to return home. Her pleas just enraged Ali, he became more and more abusive. Ali would remind Martha that Badeel had killed others and had promised to kill her if she tried to escape. Martha still attempted to escape and attempted suicide. Ali responded by taking more extreme measures. He also became more brutal in his sexual desires toward her.

She had planned her own suicide and had decided that because of the lack of means, she was going to have to smother herself with her pillow. So, Martha put her face in her pillow, then put the satin pillow case over the pillow and her head. Martha laid down and waited for death. She entertained thoughts about seeing her brother and grandparents in heaven. She wanted to escape the pain and to wake up in a much better place. The next morning, she woke up in her bed with her head still in her pillow. She became determined to try again with a different means.

She knew she would have to ask Joy, who she thought of as "Badeel's brown-nosed wife," for a favor. Forcing a smile, she asked her, "Joy, can I please look at a calendar. I know you believe in positive energy, and I do too. I need to know what day my mother's birthday is on this year, so I can send her good thoughts that day."

"I'll make a deal with you, Martha," said Joy. "If you help me clean up this room, I'll get you a calendar, but you cannot tell Ali. Ali requires that you live in want until you know submission."

"Want? Then why all of this?" Martha said, looking around the room. "These things in this room are of high quality."

"Yes, but you are also one of these things," Joy explained. These things are not really yours, you and these things belong to him. You are like a person stranded in the desert, not knowing where you are, what day it is, or what you will drink or eat. You are totally dependent on the goodwill of your master, Martha. You are merely a possession."

"Joy, you are right, I feel totally lost, but please, get me the calendar," Martha pleaded. "I will clean whatever you want me to clean. And I will never tell Ali, and I tell you I will never submit to him."

"Martha, these men are Iranian, they are extremist," she explained. "They just think different about everything, from something so simple as bread to the complex woman. It would be better if you try to understand and just be agreeable."

Martha noticed how solemn and distant Joy appeared. She is not a captive like me. She can come and go as she wants, but she seems so heavy hearted.

Joy did bring Martha the calendar the next day, and after, Martha kept her promise and helped Joy clean.

Once Martha was alone, she went to the Bristol table to look at the calendar. She sat there, looking for the best day to end her suffering. Hmm, she thought, the next Friday, Joy will stay home like she does every Friday to be with her son. So, this Friday will be the best day for me to attempt suicide again. Martha sat, counting the days. Then she noticed something. "Oh, I have not had my period for a month, and I've been sick in the mornings. I have never been late, I always know when I will start to the day." That was when she had her ah-ha moment, she was pregnant.

Martha hid her pregnancy and often blamed her symptoms on feeling home-sick or the flu. Martha struggled to keep her secret. She stayed in bed when Joy was present, knowing that Joy was the only person that would notice. Martha only ate modestly. She limited her meals to meats, fruits, and vegetables. She would flush most of her food in the toilet. She kept her weight down. During the last two months of her pregnancy, Ali went to Iran, and Badeel moved in the house. Martha was left to herself most of those days. Martha was thankful. Ali being gone was a blessing. She did not have to suffer from his wantonness. His absence also gave her the opportunity to give birth in the privacy of her segregated quarters without anyone interfering or even being aware.

Once the baby was born, she had a reason to live and to save her child. So, she allowed herself to be imprisoned while she fulfilled her role as Snow's mother. In fact, she had often thought that her role as a mother dictated what she could do and how far to take things. She had ruled out suicide. She still desired to look at possibilities for freedom as long as they would include Snow.

One night, she almost talked with a person. She thought about the night Ali had allowed Snow to order the pizza. She had observed the initial conversation between Snow and Ali. That night, she knew Ali was busy in his study with his networking. She could not resist the opportunity for a chance for them both to be free. When she heard the gate buzzer, she started down stairs.

Of course, Ali had given her an injection earlier that night. She felt off balance but also determined to ask for help, but before she had made it half way down the stairs, Ali grabbed her and pulled her back upstairs.

Ali did not gamble. If he knew any outsiders might come into the residence, she was drugged. Ali knew it was imperative that she would always be seen as the insane wife. The wife that Ali was devoted to by anyone that might see her.

However, Ali's inner circle knew the truth. There was Joy, who pretended to be blind to her forced captivity. Badeel, who always was looking for a chance to get rid of her by killing her. And then the doctor, who also pretend to be blind to her fate. She found no help from anyone. So, she devoted herself to prayer and her studies. At least Ali was a scholar and permitted her to have any books she wanted. History, science, math, all the old masters, and the new more brilliant classical novels. Martha educated herself and waited until she could use her knowledge to avenge Snow and herself.

Chapter Twelve

Ali's Life and Regrets

Ali sat in his own home on Westmoreland. He had designed and built his own fortress. He was able to monitor who came in, where they went to, and when they left his estate. He could observe all visitors and identify all possible threats. His home was full of small corridors that led from adjacent rooms throughout the house, all leading to passages that led to the outside of the home. Some led blocks away. When he envisioned the safe room, he incorporated protection from bombing, tornadoes, police, mobs, and all kinds of diverse disasters. He also became very creative in the structure, plumbing, and interior of the safe room. He installed all of the technology he could in order to survive. He knew he would be able to survive for an unlimited time with the sources he had required: water, power, ventilation, microwave, and plenty of survival foods. Ali thought of everything: sound proofing, lock down capabilities, and an escape tunnel. Ali looked around at all he had built and had done as a man in his early 40's.

For the last 48 months, Ali worked on putting his plan in place. He was going back to Iran and was taking Martha with him. He, of course, would spend a half year in the USA and the other half of the year in Iran. Once Martha left the USA with him, she would never set foot back on its soil. He had the papers, his finances, tickets, clothing, and every other detail in place for his and Martha's departure from America to his home in Iran. He knew he would have to make amends to Badeel, but his father would embrace him, even Martha will be better. She will have more freedom, she will be allowed to move freely within his home, neighborhood, town, all will know she is a captive wife, and there will be no consequence to him, it is perfectly legal. She, of course, will be hated, she is an American and the wife of Ali, so many other women had wanted to be my wife, he thought, but there was nothing, no feeling, no connection, just nothing. Ali didn't want a wife with complications. He had witnessed how his mother lived and died as a wife, a wife who was told by the law she could get a divorce. But that's not the case for a captive wife, they have no rights, could not seek a divorce, custody, or any other benefit that other wives may attempt to gain. Although, in most cases, the husband is always on the favorable side of the law anyway, even able to bend the truth, his dead mother could attest to that. I should not have so many regrets, he thought. His mind went back to Aabidah, his mother.

Ali's first regret, "If only I had been stronger, I could have fought, then maybe things would have been different." Ali grew up in a small village in Iran. He was born to Omar Mohammed Hame Ali and Aabidah Ahearan. Aabidah was the second and youngest wife of Omar. During the early part of their marriage, Omar and Aabidah seemed happy. Aabidah came from a good Muslim family with a very large dowry from her father's house. Ali was happy and would often say, "I'm the happiest of all boys." And he was until the age of seven.

During Ali's seventh year, things started to change. His mother began to complain more and more about being mistreated by Omar. It was like any nightmare, it just got worse and became darker as the nights went on. Her complaints grew into claims of abuse.

Finally, Aabidah knew she had to find help. Seeking support, she went to ask for help from her sister wife, Aliyah. Aliyah was the first wife of Omar. Aabidah thought because she was older, she would know what to do. However, Aabidah was unaware how bitter Aliyah's feelings were toward her. When Aabidah came to Aliyah for help, she took delight in simply denying or knowing anything about Omar being abusive.

The younger and naive Aabidah asked Aliyah, "How can a woman stop her husband from hitting her?"

Aliyah replied, "I do not understand what you are talking about and who you are talking about."

Aabidah replied, "I'm talking about me. Surely, you understand that Omar is mistreating me. He is hurting me, and I have begged him to stop. And it just keeps getting worse."

Although Aliyah knew exactly what Aabidah was talking about because she had saw some of it take place, and she also had firsthand knowledge because she, too, was one of Omar's victims. She, herself, had suffered beatings, but she lied and hid the truth just as she had done for years. Aliyah merely smiled and said, "Bad wives need to be beat." After that encounter, Aabidah felt discouraged and decided if she didn't have support in her house, she would go outside to find others to help her.

Aabidah followed the prescribed law by first going to her doctor to show proof of the abuse she was suffering from Omar. But she got no real help there. The doctor told her she was fine and would recover quickly. Then he sent her on to the Iman. The Iman advised her to try to make peace and to please her husband by being a good wife and mother. She then turned to the other women in the village to ask for support and to find out how she could stop being beaten by her husband. The women shook their heads and shrugged, but one of the women who had befriended her when she had first arrived from her father's house to the village told her she would need to get the divorce decree. "If you are his wife, he has the right to beat you, and he might even start to beat your little boy. All you can do is divorce him. Then when you are not his wife, he cannot legally beat you anymore."

When Aliyah heard the gossip about Aabidah, she was just too happy to inform her husband about Aabidah's activities. Omar became enraged with Aabidah. Omar confronted Aabidah with all he had learned from Aliyah. Things escalated until he hit Aabidah. She screamed at Omar that she was divorcing him. Omar was a proud man and did not want to go through the humiliation of a divorce. There also was the dowry, and he did not want to give that up either.

Omar first attempted to heal his relationship with Aabidah, but she told him it was too late and that, "Now my husband, I do not want to be married, and now at this time, I only want a divorce from you."

The inner workings of his relationships became entangled. The more he attempted to appease Aabidah, the more she persisted about the divorce. As he became more and more persistent to change her mind, he became more saddened. The more depressed he became, the more Aliyah complained about Aabidah and pointed to her as a betrayer and the source of the misery. Within weeks, Omar was committed to," no divorce ever," and so he went in search of advice himself. Aliyah suggested he talked with her brother, Mohammed. After leaving Mohammed and listening to his hateful speech, Omar was persuaded that Aabidah must have a lover if she was so set on the divorce.

And so he launched his own campaign. He became even more abusive toward Aabidah. And her demands for divorce were met with accusation. Instead of Omar agreeing to a divorce, Aabidah found herself accused of infidelity. When the charges were finally bought forth, she was accused of having sex with her brother-in-law, Mohammed. Aabidah proclaimed her innocence, stating she had always been a loyal wife and that she just didn't want to get beat. She said that she had despised Mohammed because he was so cruel to women and children. In the end, Mohammed agreed to be the witness that Omar needed to confirm his right to put Aabidah to death.

During an afternoon like any other day, she was dragged out of her home by Omar and Mohammed into the street. The men yelled out all their allegations and accusations. The mob of indignation men rushed Aabidah and threw her in the hole they had dug for her earlier. Ali and Badeel both were made to witness the stoning. Ali felt a warm tear run down his cheek, Badeel threw a stone.

Ali's little heart was broken, he swore he would never forget his mother. Ali also promised her he would never treat any living being the way his mother was treated and killed. Ali felt alone, and to make things worse, he began to be bullied by some of the other children. They called him a bastard and threw rocks at him.

Omar gave Ali to his first wife, Aliyah, to raise as her son. Aliyah was delighted. She now had a way to reach past the grave to continue to torture Aabidah through her son. Aliyah had always been jealous over Aabidah since the first day she saw her. Aabidah was beautiful with gorgeous, big green eyes and lustrous black hair. Aliyah was short with brown eyes and stiff brown hair. She let her jealousy move her to envy and to look for fault in most everything Aabidah said or did. Once, when Omar was on his rant about the Jews, he had told his family that they must always be on guard against the Jews. And that the Jews were known to sneak in the house of good Muslims and to slaughter the children while they slept in their own beds.

Aabidah, wanting to calm the children, merely stated, "Listen children, don't be scared. The Jewish people's God won't let them harm animals without a cause, so if they can't hurt animals, they won't hurt innocent children like you."

Aliyah used this claim to say that Aabidah sided with the Jews. That she deliberately undermined Omar and that she was bold enough to tell the children that Omar lied to them. Aliyah, in fact, was the person responsible for turning Omar against his second wife. And Aliyah took any opportunity to make accusations against Aabidah. She would twist and turn the truth until the lie sounded more like the truth and then she just continued to pile them up against her. So now she acted the same way toward Ali, making accusations against him, spreading rumors about him, whispering and letting lies lie in the air. Aliyah was able to drive a distance between the son and the father, all the while she strengthened Badeel to Omar. Aliyah made it her mission to destroy Ali's relationship with Omar and promote her son as the loyal son.

When Ali reached 14, he was the head of his class. His father was pleased with the good grades he made. Ali was so delighted, he found his father's approval in the hard work he did at school. So, he dove into his studies, studying for long hours into the night. He pressed on to only get A's.

At the age of 15, he forgot what his mother's beautiful face looked like. The old memories of his mother had diminished, and he could not remember his mother's sweet voice or the songs she sang or the stories she read to him as a child.

Aliyah not only destroyed the relationship between Ali and Omar but also destroyed Ali's vision of his mother. Aliyah was in control of Ali. His needs and wants had to be met through a woman that despised him and his mother. Aliyah took joy in making Ali beg her for what he needed. During one meal with the other children, she would not let him eat until he confessed that his mother was a whore and that he was a bastard.

After Ali repeated that his mother was a whore and that he was a bastard, she just laughed at him and said, "Ali, why are you not eating my good food that I cook for you." After years of being made to beg for a piece of bread from Aliyah, he forgot the fine meals that his mother Aabidah used to cook for him. Ali had a lot of hurt, and his hurt turned to anger, then his anger turned toward the one that was not there to protect him. "Why couldn't my mother have tried harder to please my father? And now, because of her, I have to work twice as hard as Badeel to prove my worth."

Ali came to the USA at the age of 20. He landed on the shore with his father's blessing and a large fortune, his mother's dowry. By law, the dowry went to Ali when he left his father's house. Ali finished his studies and became a pharmacist. He agreed to stay in the USA, to continue to work and build the hidden Islamic network in the once gateway to the West. Ali saw Missouri as a gate way for the East.

Ali thought that the West lacked real community, brotherhood, sisterhood, and the connection to family. Ali's childhood had educated him on deceit and trickery. He grew up disillusioned with the human race. Ali sought after power and control, he needed to be surrounded with layers of money and men in powerful positions.

Once, a close friend persuaded him to accompany him to a meeting he was having with Abdulla Yusuf Azzam . His friend was highly skilled in technical circuitry and Al-Qaeda was recruiting. After the meeting, Ali's friend wanted to know if he was impressed with the leader. Ali told him, "No, I was not impressed by sitting on the hard ground, and I thought that maybe this leader had puppet strings. The only thing that captivated my attention at all was when he discussed the fact that his fighters are able to take their enemies captive and that they can make captive wives out of the women."

Ali disclosed that he had a secret desire, "I want a captive wife, so I have all the control over her and she has none. Yes, my friend, I'm fascinated with the thought of owning a wife." Ali went on to say, "I do not want to die, but I will work for my beliefs and that of our brothers. No, this Al-Qaeda is not for me, my friend. I think we will find more happiness in our own dreams and work. We come from wealthy educated families. We will pull the strings and not dance. The world is changing. Islam has its foot print in the west. The Romans laid down roads as a foundation to bring civilization together and to conqueror the world as they knew it then. And we Iranians will establish networks and connections that will give us the pathway to tear down fundamental beliefs of the West. We will blow up the roads and tear down what the Roman Empire inspired. We aspire to destroy by submission or by death. We will dominate the world, a world without Jews, Roman Catholics, Christians, and Hindus. Our mission is to inject terror and chaos. And I will work to build the sleeper cells and the underground in America."

His friend then told him, "I will stay here. We will always be brothers joined to fight the same enemy. I will join Al-Qaeda and give them my skills. I will play the fiddle, I will not dance, I will be greater than Azzam, you will see."

Ali's second regret was why he did not wait until he was back in Iran to find his wife. Ali was not sure if the safe room led to his desire to have a captive American wife, or if he just always had the desire for a captive wife. So, he designed the safe room as such. Whichever was the original intent, the end results were the same.

"Why was I there in that spot when she fell? Why did I feel the need to help her up and then why did I keep going back?" he questioned himself. "Yes, there was something about her that hit an inner string and brought me to my knees when I looked at her. The connection had to be related to his mother, he thought. "No woman has ever held my attention like that. Why did I allow those fantasies to take root in my mind? If I had been in Iran, I could have asked her father for her. He would have also given me a large dowry. This cursed America! The women are traps, dressed up to lure a good man."

He remembered that he had needed the help from Badeel, and Badeel has vowed to kill her if she ever tried to escape. He remembered that Badeel made him promise that one day he would want something too, and Ali would help him get it whatever it was. And yes, Badeel held him to that promise. But he had wanted Martha to be his wife, and Badeel's ruthless character had helped him get her and keep her.

And I was wrong about her, he thought. I had planned on keeping her a prisoner only until she agreed to marry me. I knew it would take time. After all, American women were inferior to Iranian women and that they were immature. And this woman, all she did was cry and plead and refuse me! If I had acted sooner and obtained that fake passport for her the first month, we would be in Iran, and things would have been different. Then Snow was born. He remembered how the news of the baby, his baby, froze him. I didn't know what to do, so I did nothing, he thought. Then his mind went back to the first night he saw his baby, his little Snow.

"Why did Allah let me stay in Iran during those months leading up to Snow's birth, he wondered. I knew I had been in Iran too long, but I needed to see my father and my family. And it took me weeks searching for the right property and the right house. And I did find the house, it was in my mother's village, a house for me and Martha. I remember the day I bought it. I had visited with my mother's sister. I was taken back in my mind to my childhood, and I remembered how much love we had shared. I told my aunt I was married to an American woman. I listened and had hope when she said, "Ali, once you bring her to Iran, she will become like other wives. She will submit to you, her husband, and to Allah." I was determined to change things between myself and Martha. I had wanted to talk to her when I first came back from Iran. But being back in Iran stirred old memories and old pains had arisen up in me. So, I did what I always do, just a few drinks to clear my head.

Ali did have a few drinks and those led to more drinks. He didn't remember becoming intoxicated. He membered going to Martha's room and Martha rejecting him, as always. The drunken, enraged Ali was going to make her pay. After all, she was his only effective punching bag. Then he saw that tiny thing, not sure at first what it was. Then Martha yelled at him, that was a shock, but what she said hit hard, "YOUR BABY!" He was shocked, and he stayed in that state for weeks.

Ali used the birth of Snow for his ends, too. He remembered his childhood and how the women in his father's house treated children. He realized he might have more control over Martha by allowing her to keep her baby close to her. "My daughter Snow was no regret," he reasoned. "We had a real bond like a child and father should. And she honored me for most of her youth, if only she had been raised in Iran, she would have totally submitted to me, and she would have learned not to question my authority." He remembered how fierce Badeel pleaded with him to forcefully take the baby and give it to Joy to raise. But really, he could not have left that little baby go or her mother.

I love my daughter, but she has been gone for two years now, his thoughts went on, I was almost happy before the betrayal. Yes, before the night that Martha had that taxi drive Snow away. Martha has no idea about honor and family. She lives uninformed, uncaring, a hateful Catholic, and as a capitalist. I trapped myself here in this land of my enemies, and I trapped myself with needing to keep Martha. As much as I hate this weakness, I will never let her go. My desires for her hold me captive but then I hate her for causing me to lose Snow. Sometimes I think that I suffer more than she does, and at times I wonder who is the real captive?

The third regret, I made a promise to my brother, whatever you ask of me, I will do for you, he remembered. I want this woman, and I need your help to take her and keep her. I needed my brother's help because my lust overwhelmed me. I would have agreed to anything. Then, after I took Martha, I found that I needed someone to help run the house and keep Martha's presence there quiet. I could not trust any outsider. Badeel was married to an American woman named Joy. They had a son together. Badeel had planned on taking Joy and his son with him when he went back to Iran. But Badeel, again, helped me.

He could hear Badeel's words as plain as he did so many years past, "I will leave my wife here until you finish with our affairs here. She will help you with all you need. You will not have to worry, she will never let the secrets of this house be known. She can work here for you during the day and return home at night and continue to live in my house with my son. Someday we will all live in Iran together with our American wives. Don't worry, my brother."

And Badeel was true to his word. Joy continued to work for me and help as needed, both with Martha and with Snow. But the dark day came, that day when Badeel wanted to cash in his chips. So he told me, "Ali, I have decided what I want for my payment, I want to wed Snow!"

I tried to reason with Badeel for Snow. I told him, "No, Badeel, Snow is so young, and she is your niece. What did our father say about this, Badeel? This is too much that you ask. You want my young daughter?"

"Ali, you know our father," he said. "That this is not uncommon for a man to marry a younger niece. He also agrees with me that I should consummate the marriage now. Agree to keep your oath to me. Give me your daughter. I will take her as my wife and strengthen our bond. You have pledged to give me what I ask of you on the day I ask. Is this not true? So, then it is in my power to decide when I should lay with her and take her virginity."

She was only nine, he continued to remiss. Perhaps I should have refused to give Badeel my approval when he claimed his rights to Snow as a child bride. I was not at ease with this, and I attempted to persuade him to wait. I told my brother to wait until she was 13. But he would not agree, his way prevailed. He argued that, "This was not uncommon in our country. This happens often, and it is part of our beliefs." But why my Snow, why did it have to happen to her? And Snow did change after that. But once Martha comforted her and gave her those dolls, she seemed to have recovered.

Regret four, not sending Snow to Iran with Badeel. Women must be married and be married to a man with money and means, he reasoned. And I waited too long to send Snow to Iran. I had listened to advice of women and my own desire to keep Snow with me for a little longer. I lost her and I lost face with Badeel. I know Snow would have flourished in Iran. Iran is going to be the most powerful nation in the world, and I wanted her in a house rooted there. Now she is gone! I have waited two years for Snow's return, but no news. The men in my network could not help me, there was no trace of her. It as if Snow no longer existed. Maybe she had died. She was accidently injected with the concoction I prepared especially for Martha. Martha's tolerance is high, she needed the higher dosage, but it could probably have killed Snow, but there were no reports of anyone finding her dead or alive.

Throughout the years she was gone, Ali's mind would go back to the day Snow left, somehow wanting to change it. He remembered the lie he had told Mr. Graham that day. He often pretended that his lie was true. Then his mind would go back to the day he lost Snow. He had opened the gate for Mr. Graham to come in. After only a few minutes, he remembered how he had caught a glimpse over Graham's shoulders, of Martha and Snow running through the grounds towards the gate from the window. He remembered the panic he felt and how he even surprised himself with how calm his voice sounded when he said, "Mr. Graham, please wait while I attend to my sick wife."

He remembered running frantically through the tunnel and intercepting Martha about a block away. He visually recalled how he ended up struggling with both of them and how he accidently injected Snow with the mixture he had made for Martha. He remembered how he had to watch as the cab took Snow away, how he hit Martha to knock her out, and how he carried her back to the house. He hastily chained her back to her bed. How easily he was able to compose himself. He remembered how his heart was pounding within his chest as he walked back to the formal room where he had left Mr. Graham. He recalled seeing a patient and unaware Mr. Graham merely looking at some papers from his brief case.

"I am so sorry I kept you waiting, but as you know, my wife is very ill. She just had a horrible episode," he explained. "So, what can I help you with, Mr. Graham?"

"Well, I came in response to your letter asking me to come to your home tonight after school was out," he calmly replied. "I did note that Snow had missed school today."

Ali remembered how quick his thinking was when he first spoke the lie. "Yes, that is right. I did ask you to come to the house," he told him. "I wanted to inform you that I needed to pull Snow out of school. As you were a witness tonight, you can see that her mother is very ill. I must devote hours to comfort and give my wife the care she needs. I also have to think about Snow's best interest, so I have sent her to Iran to live with my family there. Is there anything I need to do or forms I need to complete or sign?"

"Yes, we have a withdrawal form," he explained. "If you could complete that and sign it, that will be all that is needed. Also, if you could let us know what school she will be attending, we will send her records there."

"Mr. Graham, girls do not attend school in Iran. But I will sign your forms. Please have them mailed or faxed to me, and I will sign them."

"Of course, Mr. Hame, I will get them to you by tomorrow morning."

Ali also remembered how he broke down after Mr. Graham left. He wanted the lie he told to Mr. Graham to be the truth. And how throughout the years that followed, he would allow himself time to imagine Snow was safe in Iran. But then the truth would invade his thoughts, and he knew she was gone, most likely no longer among the living.

Ali never recovered from his loss of Snow. He saw Aabidah in Snow, and now that she was gone, memories of his mother were triggered in his mind. He not only suffered and grieved for Snow but also for his mother and her death. The voice in his head grew stronger. The voice told him to be merciful and told him to be a better man. Aabidah was the voice in his head, and with time, it grew louder. Yes, he missed his home, and it would not be long until he would again see the beauty of his country. Once home, he will receive much honor. If he delayed and got caught, he would be labeled as a kidnapper, a criminal, a radical. No, it was time, he would return to Iran now. He wished with all his heart that Snow was in Iran, knowing she was not. Ali felt the same pain he did Valentine's day, the day he lost his only child and the only person that really loved him.

Regret five. "Yes, I regret beating Martha the night she deceived me and attempted to run," he said to himself. "I could not control my anger, I lost control. I thought I had killed my own daughter, and maybe I did kill Snow. And so, I beat Martha and kept hitting her. I was too hard, if I had known that there was another baby in her womb, my baby, I would not had beat her at all."

Chapter Thirteen

A Friend in Joy

Joy was taken aback when she walked into Martha's room on that Valentine's night, the day Snow disappeared. "Oh, Martha, he has really hurt you bad this time!" Joy said as she examined Martha.

Martha began to have cramps, the cramps continued to increase in their intensity. The pain became unbearable. Then she began to bleed, it was a miscarriage!

"Martha, you have had a miscarriage," Joy said. "I think you will be okay. The whips cuts did not go too deep. I know you are hurting, but we can take care of this ourselves. We won't call that horrible, unfit doctor. You will heal, you will see. I know you might not want to hear this, but Ali probably saved your life. Badeel wanted to shoot you, but Ali refused to give him permission. He told Badeel that he would whip you and punish you. Well, now my journey has changed again. Omar and I will be staying here. Badeel had planned on taking all three of us to Iran, but now he said I must stay here for at least a year. Martha, I know you love Snow, but I had wanted her to come with us. I would had taken care of her just as if she was my daughter. We would had been sister wives forever. She would had been given a high status in a very wealthy home."

Martha, in a shaky, quivering voice, asked, "Has anyone heard from Snow?"

"No, Martha," she replied. "Ali was afraid the injection may have killed her. He said it was a strong one because you have such a high tolerance rate, but there was no news. Ali is talking with all of his connections and there is nothing, just nothing. Stay strong, Martha, I know you could not help but try to escape with Snow. But you will never be free. Ali takes such extreme precautions. You are doomed to be a captive wife, and I'm doomed to be the first wife to Badeel." Joy finished cleaning up the blood, changing the sheets, and removing the fetus. "I'll see you tomorrow," she said when she finished.

But Martha did not get better. There were complications from the miscarriage, excessive prolonged bleeding, extreme cramping, then she began to have a fever. When Joy came to tend to Martha, she found her nonresponsive. Joy called out to Ali, "Call that so-called doctor! You must hurry."

Martha had slipped away and was on her own journey through the bright tunnel. She awoke in a beautiful place. She had arrived in heaven. She was so peaceful. The crystal river was flowing before her. She heard beautiful singing, and when she looked down, it was all flowers. People she somehow knew all surrounded her as they came to welcome her. She gasped when she saw her grandparents. Then a beautiful eastern woman approached her. She had luscious black hair and huge eyes. But it was what was laying in her arms that drew Martha's attention. Martha's heart leapt, the woman did not say words out loud, but they were able to converse through thoughts.

"Hello, Martha, this is your baby. What will you call him, Martha, what is his name?"

"His name will be Jack, after my father," she said.

"Oh, what a perfect name, he looks like a Jack," the woman replied.

"And who are you, what is your name?" asked Martha.

"My name is Aabidah," she told her.

SNOW AT THE DOME

Then Martha was unable to keep looking at the woman holding Jack. A light shone so bright from a man that suddenly was standing next to her. He smiled at her. She heard his words like thunder.

"You have been faithful and have endured much. You can go back if you want. There is still much more suffering ahead there. But one day, you will be back on the other side of your suffering. Snow is not here, she waits for you back there. If you go back, remember, this is your reward, and when you are called back next time, you will stay."

Martha was suddenly slammed back into her body. The pain was unbearable. She heard the doctor's words. "She is stable, so the transfusion seems to have worked. She should recover."

Joy smiled and so did the so-called doctor as he closed the door behind him. Joy continued to visit and take care of Martha. Daily, she would tend to Martha, and as time went on, Martha and Joy became allies. Martha changed also. Because of her near-death experience, she decided to live in the moment, especially the good ones. One day after Martha had healed, Joy came in Martha's room in a very happy mood. She was singing and then she started to dance around the room. Joy was belly dancing, and she grabbed Martha's hands and pulled her up. "Let's dance," she declared.

"No," said Martha. "I don't know how to dance like that, besides, it looks suggestive."

"It is fun," replied Joy, "come on, it's like floating."

Martha decided to give it a try, so she joined in, and to her surprise, it felt good, it was fun! So, Martha began to learn how to belly dance. Soon, she was singing and dancing with Joy. Martha mentioned one day to Joy that she had taken piano lessons. "You know, Joy, I have not thought about music or about playing the piano for a long time, and I'm pretty good. I can sing, too."

"Wow, that is great," Joy responded. "I'm going to talk to Ali. You need to have a keyboard at least. How much fun will that be?"

Martha went on, "I don't know, but I would love to be able to play music and sing again." The next day, Joy brought the key board into Martha's room. The women were overjoyed as Martha played and they sang. Martha was really good.

Joy would spend two more years in America before going to Iran. The house became more tolerable. Before Joy departed for Iran, she gave Martha control over her life. One day, while she was getting supplies for Martha's wounds, she took a bottle of sedatives with her. She showed them to Martha and advised Martha to keep them hidden in a secure place as Joy cut Martha's mattress and hid the bottle of sedatives inside.

In the months that followed, Martha did not use the sedatives to escape life, suicide was not an option. Although she did not know what had happened to her Snow, she believed in her heart that there was hope and she clung to that hope. I will remain here for when she comes back. I will continue to pray and to gain knowledge, and I will be ready for that day, she told herself.

Ali decided to add more security to the house, so he added cameras and video. He sealed the front door to the safe room. and he extended the hidden corridor from the study to the safe room. He also reinforced the underground tunnel that ran under the street to the other side of the neighbor's. If he was alerted, he would use the hidden passageway to go into the safe room. And if ever there was another incident of encroachment, he could past through the tunnel to the outside.

Chapter Fourteen

Getting to Know You

After reading the letter that he had taken out of the lining of the coat, Dr. Sunn called his mentor and colleague, Dr. Rose. Dr. Rose immediately came to the hospital. Dr. Sunn slowly handed Dr. Rose the letter that Martha had wrote three years prior.

Dr. Rose murmured, "Little Martha!" after reading it.

Dr. Sunn then handed the blue coat to Dr. Rose. "Yes, this is the coat Martha was wearing when she disappeared 17 years ago."

"Get me the phone, please," Dr. Rose asked him. I am going to call Jack and Anna. They are in their late 50's. I think it is best to have them here when we inform them of this letter. And then we need to move quickly as Martha asked us to do three years ago. How is Snow doing, Dr. Sunn?"

"She is still in a catatonic state," he replied.

"Well, Dr. Sunn, maybe we can jog her sub conscious with reality?" suggested Dr. Rose

The DuTro's were there in what seemed like only moments. Anna crumbled to the floor when she was presented with the blue Toscana coat. Dr. Rose handed Jack the letter. Upon reading the letter, an obviously upset Jack exclaimed, "I'm going there now!"

"Please, remain calm and just breathe a few deep breaths," said Dr. Rose while putting his arm around Jack's shoulder.

Dr. Sunn assured the family that the authorities were on their way with a SWAT team to the address given in the letter.

Dr. Sunn walked over to Anna and took her hand and said, "Anna, do you think you can handle another revelation?"

"Good or bad?" asked Anna hesitantly.

"Good," replied Dr. Sunn and then added, "but some bad."

"Just go on, we are pretty strong," she replied. "Tell us, please. We need to know everything. No one can understand what we have been through with a missing child unless they have had the same heartbreak."

Dr. Rose smiled at Jack and asked, "Do you have a cigar?"

"What does that have to do with anything, old friend?" he asked.

"Well, we believe that Martha has a daughter. The girl's name is Snow. She is not in very stable condition right now, but it has to be the Snow that Martha talked about in her letter."

Anna and Jack both looked puzzled.

Dr. Rose said with a smile, "Snow is here just down the hall, are you ready to meet her? But you must prepare yourself, she is not well, as I have said."

Jack and Anna walked into the group room and was directed to a table where a green-eyed girl sat. She looked as if she was in an altered-state.

"Hello, Snow," said Dr. Sunn, "these are your grandparents, Jack and Anna DuTro."

Snow continued to carry on as before. Looking at nothing and grabbing hold of air, smiling and giggling.

Anna was the first to speak, "She resembles Martha, but with a darker complexion."

Jack said, "She looks more like our boy, Kenneth."

"Can we hug her?" asked Anna.

"Yes, of course," replied Dr. Rose.

Anna approached Snow and gave her a big hug. Jack put his arm around her, and smiling, he gave her a comforting pat. Snow did not respond, she just stayed in the same state.

Dr. Rose asked Anna, "Do you have a photo of Martha?"

Anna opened her purse and pulled out a picture. "This was the last school picture taken of Martha," replied Anna. Anna put the photo in Snow's hand. "Please look, Snow, this is our daughter who was taken from us when she was 13. Could she be your mother?"

As Snow's eyes locked on the photo, she stopped making any movement or noise. Everyone just stood there in the moment, waiting in total silence.

Being triggered by the photo, Snow screamed out, "I'm not Snow, my name is Aunty Kay."

Dr. Rose led the now confused DuTros to the executive office suite, promising an explanation. Dr. Sunn motioned to Aunty Kay to follow. Once everyone was in the office, Dr. Rose attempted to explain the hospital's work with Snow.

Then Aunty Kay startled everyone again by snarling out, "Who, what, where, there's not a Snow anywhere, just lovely me, Aunty Kay. And I'm demanding to be released immediately. Do you hear me?"

Anna stood with a down cast look, "I've just learned I have a granddaughter named Snow, now she's claiming her name is Aunty Kay. Can one of you good doctors shine some light on what is going on here?"

Dr. Sunn said, "Of course," clearing his throat. He looked at Aunty Kay and asked, "Aunty Kay, let your biological grandparents decide about you being released after you answer a few questions for me."

Aunty Kay shrugged her shoulders.

"Aunty Kay, please tell us, what is your nationality, and what is your age?"

Aunty Kay replied, "I am Asian and I'm 54. What does that have to do with releasing me from this stinking hospital?"

Anna, eyes widened and with a knowing head shake at Dr. Sunn, said, "I see. We hope you start feeling better soon, hon, but you're in a good place here with these good doctors."

Dr. Sunn called for an orderly to take Snow back to her room. Aunty Kay left without any other disruption.

Chapter Fourteen

Can We Talk?

When the officials arrived on Westmoreland Place, the house was empty. The police were not able to detect a living being in the home. They spread out through the house and grounds, inspecting every inch. They were searching, looking for any evidence and/or DNA left behind. However, they did not discover the safe room, thus they were unable to pass into the concealed hideaway.

Ten minutes before SWAT arrived, Ali was in bed when he was awakened by a phone call from one of his associates. He was informed that the officials were on their way. He sprang into action, awakening Martha and ordering her to his study, and then on through the passageway to the safe room. He only gave Martha enough time to gather some clothes, a book, and a few of her belongings. Martha also grabbed what she had kept hidden for many months, the gift that Joy had given her.

Ali felt secure in the safe room. He knew there was no reason to fear anything. The officials would never find them in the safe room, and no one would be able to penetrate into the massive, hidden room. Ali also had his fortune, he had Aabidah's dowry, papers, and documentation. His brother had given him the identity of a deceased woman.

She had been of American and Iranian heritage. Ali also had a burqa for Martha to wear during the long jet ride to Iran. He had thought of everything.

Once in the safe room, Ali turned toward Martha and spoke, "I wish to speak with you. We can no longer stay here. This country is no longer safe for me. Martha, you have been my captive wife for many years, and I have been your captive in return, trying to figure out how to keep you. When I first saw you, I had emotions I haven't felt for years. When I walked you home that first day, your singing and dancing moved me, and I wanted you more than anything I had ever wanted. I did use you as a sexual object for my own desires. I was the captive, my mind and lust kept me a prisoner of my own corrupted selfishness. Please, forgive me. Martha, you can never understand. My world is so different from yours. We are not cuddled children as children are here in your country. My childhood was horrific. I was forced to witness my mother's stoning. There was no one I could turn to. I was the only child my mother had. I don't think I ever had time to grieve her. After her death, my father gave me to his first wife to raise, and that is where I lived until I left Iran. This woman hated my mother and was the tool of her demise. This woman debased me, ridiculed me, and turned my father against me!"

Martha sat listening and amazed. Ali might have a heart after all, she thought. "Go on, Ali," she said in a monotone voice.

Ali continued, "I had to wall up any emotions, so no one could see any weakness in me. I did not experience any feelings. I put on and wore emotional armor, which I have continued to wear since my childhood. Martha, our Snow pierced into my armor. Her eyes held love like my mother's eyes. Snow reminded me of my loyalty and love for Aabidah, my mother. Besides my mother, I don't think anyone has ever loved me or deeply cared for me. My brother and I are loyal to each other, we would die for each other, but that is the code we live by. But having a daughter and a family was true love. I felt empty and had the same lonely feeling of rejection I had growing up in Iran with Aliyah. I felt like you took my world away, and once again, I felt unwanted with no family. This caused me to become so undone in my thinking. When I lost Snow, I blamed you. I raged and lost control, I ask you to forgive me for beating you so badly. When I caused you to have a miscarriage, I had to face the facts. How could I have the love of a child if her mother was my captive? And then I was told that you lost the baby and almost died because of what I had done. I felt deep pain. I think that I mourned my mother's, Snow's, and the baby's death all at the same time. The pain and misery brought me to the end of my suffering. I have dealt with hidden things. I realized that I wanted a captive wife, so I would never lose her. Martha, I feel unlovable."

Martha sat, stoic, while listening to a stranger, someone she did not know at all.

Ali continued, "Martha, because I lost Snow, blood of my blood, I have changed my thoughts. Believe me, I am sorry, I have changed, and I want you to be my wife. I want to marry you. I have come to love you. I have papers and passports, we can go to Iran. I will make you my queen. You will live in lavish luxury and with honor as my wife. We can still have more children. You will have servants and your own finances. I will give you Aabidah's dowry to prove to you I have changed. There are only two things you need to do. First, denounce your Christian beliefs, and then just to say yes to my proposal. I'm now waiting your reply."

"Before I respond, tell me why you have awakened me in the middle of the night and brought me to the safe room?" questioned Martha.

Ali answered, "The officials are coming here. We must escape through the tunnel. I have transportation waiting for us as we speak. In 24 hours, we will be in Iran." Ali took out a heavy metal box. "This is full of jewels, funds, CD's, and bonds. It is a fortune, and I give it to you."

Martha forced a smile to her lips as she asked, "How can we escape from this room?"

Ali went over to the wall and pushed a switch. There was a concealed panel that opened into the room. Martha could see that there was an escape tunnel behind it.

"Oh, I see," said Martha. "Ali, we have a ritual here in America. If a man asks a woman to marry him, he kneels down to make his proposal. Will you show me that honor? If you can kneel before me and ask for my hand in marriage, I will give you my answer."

Ali was taken back, he could feel a happiness arising within him. He knelt before Martha. He also handed her the metal box. Martha took a deep breath, and with all her pent-up rage, she raised the box over her head while Ali's head was bent down, waiting to hear her say yes.

He did not hear a yes. Instead, he heard and felt a strange thud. It was his head as Martha had brought the metal box down with all her force, hitting him on top of his head. He felt a warm, hot stream of blood quickly running down his face and then everything went black. Martha looked in his jacket and found the syringe that she knew Ali had brought to inject her with if she would not comply with his desires. She mixed her sedatives with water, then added them in the syringe. She administered about a third of the mixture. She then walked over to her paper and crayons and wrote a letter. As she began to write, she was not sure if she would administer more of the mixture in his vein to kill him.

Martha grabbed a piece of paper and a crayon. Martha wrote, "Ali, I will never denounce my Savior, Jesus Christ. I know Him, and He is my best friend, and He is my King. He has been with me these past few years. When I was beaten, He comforted me. When I was close to death, He showed me heaven and what awaits me. Now, I have not decided if I will inject you with the rest of this syringe or not. I hate you and despise your very being. You stole me from my home, you have hurt the people I love. I was my father's princess and my mother's joy. They had to deal with the death of my brother, and they were not even able to grieve for me because they never knew if I was dead or alive. They still most surely are unsettled. You stole my childhood and kept me as a sex slave. You have hurt my daughter and you killed my baby with your rage. Just to let you know, I figured out your phone. I texted that excuse of a man, your brother, Badeel. I told him in the text that she is dead, I had to kill her, Martha DuTro no longer breathes air. Badeel was upset because you texted in English. The other part of his reply was asking you to find a stone and hurl it at my temple, then to spit on me and leave me to rot in the safe room.

If I decide not to kill you and you are reading this, know that your phone and all of your identity is with the officials. This is my insurance policy that you will never darken Snow or me with your presence again. If I do let you live, it is because of Jesus, but He would understand if I killed you."

She thought to herself, I need to end his life. I must do this to protect myself, Snow, and other innocent people. As she was looking at Ali's arm, she saw that the brief case had flipped over and there were papers on the floor. As she looked down at them, she saw a photo. It was a picture of the beautiful woman, the one she had seen in heaven holding her little baby Jack. Yes, of course! She is Snow's and baby Jack's grandmother, Aabidah.

Martha walked over to Ali and bent down with the syringe. She could see he was still breathing. She wiped down everything she had touched. She dropped the needle next to Ali and took a red crayon, finishing her letter with these words, 'Warning, stay away from us because if I ever see you again, I will kill you.'

Martha took Aabidah's photo, the metal box, Ali's phone, his id's, and walked into the tunnel, closing the panel behind her. She reemerged on the other side of the neighbor's yard. She then enjoyed the long walk home. She stopped at a 24-hour Walgreens as she had wanted to use a pay phone but was unable to find one. She asked the clerk if she could borrow the phone. She then called her old home phone number she never forgot.

Chapter Sixteen

Homecoming

Her mother heard the phone ring, answering the phone, Anna heard, "Mom, it is me, Martha. Please do not tell anyone but Father that I am alive, and I will be home within 30 minutes. Just wait for me, and Mom, do your focused breathing. Yes, it is really me!"

Anna and Jack waited by the door for the entire 30 minutes. Then finally, they saw Martha walking up the walkway. Once at the door, they fell into each other's arms and quickly moved into the safety of their home. In the house, they held each other, sobbing for a very long time. Finally, the family was able to compose themselves enough to talk.

"Martha, this has been a day full of emotions. We read your letter. We thought we had found you, then the police said the house was empty. We were devastated again, they attempted to encourage us as they said they would continue to look for you. But we thought you were lost again. And then you called us!" Jack said, sobbing.

"It must had been heartbreaking for you both to think you had lost another child. During the time I was captive, I often thought about my big brother, Kenny. I felt that he was often there with me, and I know if he had lived, he would have stopped Ali. Kenny is one of the reasons I fought so hard to live. I had to come back home because he didn't.

But we have to be careful. We cannot let everyone know I am here," she told them, looking at them intensely. "Martha DuTro has to die." Anna gasped, and tears filled her eyes again.

"Just listen." She then explained where she had been for so many years. She told them about the day Ali had taken her and how he kept her a captive hidden in his home. She told them about Snow and how then nine-year-old Snow was abused by Badeel as he claimed her for his child bride. They listened intently, not wanting to interrupt. She told them about what had happened when she attempted to escape with Snow. She told how she had wanted to kill Ali but didn't. How she texted Ali's brother, Badeel, pretending to be Ali himself and confessed that he had killed Martha. When she had finished, they hugged and cried more. And then they gave thanks for their daughter's return.

"Mom, I know that Snow is alive," she believed. "I figure she finally was able to tell someone, and that is why the police came to Ali's house."

Jack took his daughter's hands and looked deep into her eyes. "Yes, she is alive! We saw her. It was the letter you had wrote and hid in the blue coat, Dr. Sunn found it. He showed it to Dr. Rose, and he called us."

Martha began to shake and cry. "What about Snow, where is she?"

"Calm down," encouraged Anna, "just breathe, Martha, it's okay. We have seen Snow. Doctor Rose sent for us when they found the letter."

"Well, how is she, what did she say to you, did she tell you about me?" said Martha, frantically looking for answers.

Anna led Martha to the couch and put her arm around her, holding her very tight. "We have seen Snow, she is beautiful, but she says her name is Aunty Kay. Dr Rose and his colleague, Dr. Sunn, explained to us that Snow has been under treatment for the last three years. They said she arrived in a cab heavily drugged and was very ill. They said she has something, multiple personality disorder?"

"Oh God," cried out Martha. "What can we do to help her?"

"Let's stay calm tonight, Snow is safe," Anna told her.

They huddled together and talked late into the night, they talked about Kenneth, Snow, family, and friends.

Jack finally said, "We all need to get some rest. We will be able to think clearer if we get some sleep. Look," Jack said as he pulled the curtain back, "the night is gone, and I can see the morning light." Smiling at Martha, he said, "When you wake up, your mother will make your favorite breakfast. We will eat and then call Dr. Rose over to meet with us."

"Oh, that's a good idea, Dad," Martha said, feeling better. "We have to think this all through. I do not want the media to know anything about our business, and I want to protect Snow through all of this. Yes, I need to rest, is my bed still here?"

"Of course, honey. Your room is just like you left it," said Anna in a soft voice. "Come on, let's get some sleep," said Anna as she smiled at Martha. The family walked up the stairs to the bedrooms, gave each other another hug, and finally went to bed.

It took Martha a few minutes to realize where she was when she woke up. This isn't a dream, she thought. It's all true, I am free. She was in her old room. Everything was just as she had left it. She felt a little foolish thinking how naïve she had been in the past before Ali took her. She struggled adjusting into her own skin and who she had become. She opened a drawer on her dresser, looking for something to wear. She saw her old gym suit, folded up and neatly put away. She laughed to herself; it's like I am thinking about trying to fit into my old gym suit, and it will never fit again. No, I'm not the same innocent little girl I once was. And then she heard herself say, "Thank you GOD." She smiled, she was home, and the nightmare was over.

Or was it? She had left Ali laying on the floor after he was knocked out. She knew he was still breathing when she left, but did he continue to keep breathing? Martha quickly pulled out an old pair of sweats and a top. She hurriedly got dressed and ran downstairs to the kitchen. The kitchen looked just the same, the same yellow warming colors with white trim woodwork and white curtains. She felt warm and unafraid. Her thoughts were interrupted by an old familiar voice. She looked around and saw Dr. Rose standing in the doorway.

"Hello, Martha," he said. "We have all been broken hearted about your disappearance."

"I'm home now, Dr. Rose. I feel safe again," she told him. "I have often thought about the anguish my parents and friends were enduring, especially immediately after my abduction. How do you think they are doing now?" Martha asked, tilting her head toward her parents.

"Martha, look at them," he said. "They are busy chattering and smiling. I haven't seen them like this for years. They seem so happy again, but a lot has happened in the last couple of days."

Martha smiled and then quickly added, "I need to talk with you, but I want client privilege."

"Oh, of course. Give me a minute, Martha. Excuse me while I make this call."

Martha gave Jack and Anna a big hug as she said, "I love you guys."

"Let's eat, Martha," said Jack. "Your mom has been overjoyed because she can cook for her daughter." Smiling, he nodded his head and said, "Please, join us, Dr. Rose. Anna and I are a little tired. We could not sleep at all. We are overwhelmed that our daughter is back home. We kept sneaking over to her room while she slept, cracking the door just enough to see that she was in her bed safe and back home."

Martha ate as if she hadn't eaten in days. She savored her food and the sight of her parents. She was overjoyed, putting away any negative thoughts for the moment. During her years of being a captive, she learned to be present in each and every positive moment. The doorbell rang and it scared her, but she concealed it all very well.

Jack went to the door and greeted a man in his early 30's with a pleasant smile, "Hello, Dr. Sunn, please come in. This beautiful young woman is our wonderful Martha," added Jack.

Dr. Rose patted Dr. Sunn on the back. "I am so glad you're here.

As I informed you on the phone, Martha wants to sign consent papers before talking with us."

"I have them right here," replied Dr. Sunn as he handed a pack of paper work to Dr. Rose.

"Good, can you sit next to me, Martha, so we can review these forms and get your signature?" asked Dr. Rose.

Within a few minutes, Martha had signed the consent forms.

"Okay, now that I have client privilege, I need to talk with you Dr. Rose."

"Martha, feel comfortable to talk about anything, we want to hear what you have to say," assured Dr. Rose.

Martha looked up at Dr. Sunn with a shy, questioning look.

"Martha, Dr. Sunn also holds client privilege," assured Dr. Rose, "and he has been Snow's doctor for the past two years. He is very much aware of the issues in your family's case."

"Well, first of all, I need to tell you that I left the man who had held me his prisoner in his home. When I left him, he was still alive. I had hit him in the head with a metal box. After he fell, I injected him with a mixture of valiums, enough to keep him unconscious long enough for me to get away. I might have killed him, I'm not sure."

"Please, go on," said Dr. Rose, "you have our attention."

"I have been through hell and so has my daughter Snow because of him. Ali is so removed from being a human being. He told me about his plan before I escaped. His plan was for me to marry him and go to Iran with him. He is such a narcissistic, self-involved, just an evil man. He kidnapped, tortured, and imprisoned me for all these years and then he wanted me to go to Iran with him! Anyway, he has a lot of connections here and in Iran. He gave me a new identity as Patricia Parsi. He told me she was American and Iranian. Ali's own mother was stoned by his family, so I'm not sure what they did to Patricia. But I need her identity. I do not want to stay a victim or be treated as one. I just want a new life for myself and Snow."

They all listened intently as Martha went on.

"It is only by God's grace that I am alive today. Ali's brother, Badeel, kept me under a death threat, promising he would kill me if I tried to escape. And in all reality, Ali and Badeel did kill me. They took my youth, my innocence, the over nights with my best friends, our Sunday night dinners, the prom, dances, my first kiss! No, they killed me. I am not the Martha that Ali took from you, I have changed. Their twisted ideology killed Martha. From now on, from this moment to the end of my life, I am Patty! So, do your best to remember to call me Patty. I will stay hidden, incognito until we can figure all of this out and find a new place to live where we can start a new life."

Anna looked sad, "But Martha, I mean, Patty, I don't want to lose my daughter again."

"You won't, Mom. I'm here with you and Dad. You and Dad can adopt me. We can do the adult adoption, so legally, Patty will be your daughter. We can call your lawyer Tim and get him to draw up the adoption papers. Mom, if only there was another way but there isn't. Dad, I have Ali's phone with the text messages admitting he killed Martha. I have a message from Badeel, too, he is praising Ali for killing me. I think we should get this to the police, and I will draw the lay out of the house, so they can locate the hidden safe room. Maybe Ali is still lying there unconscious or dead, or he may be gone."

Looking stern, Jack said, "I think that we have enough to prove he kidnapped and imprisoned Martha, and we have the letter she wrote."

Nodding his head, Dr. Rose said, "We have the letter she wrote, but her letter makes mention of Snow. I think we should not let anyone else see that letter for now."

"Yes, you're absolutely right," Jack agreed.

Dr. Rose smiled at Martha and assured her," Your letter is covered under client privilege."

The discussion then took off and became intense. After the fury, they all agreed to follow Patty's wishes. The grateful Patty said, "Now, please take me to Snow."

"Mom, these clothes look bad. I think I am going to change if I can find something else."

"Come on, I'll help you," said Anna, "you men just wait, we will be right back."

Dr. Sunn, looking toward Jack, and said, "You have a very impressive and strong-willed daughter."

They all chuckled.

Patty was back within only a few minutes, "I just want to thank you all for supporting and being here for me." She then wrapped a headscarf on concealing her face. She put her sun glasses on, then followed Dr. Rose out to his BMW. She waved good bye to her parents as they stood on the porch, beaming. Patty was going to the hospital to claim her daughter. Dr. Sunn was fumbling with his keys, trying to get into his car so he could keep up.

As they neared the hospital Patty could see the gate around the grounds of the hospital. She could feel her heart beating through her chest as she was filled with so much anticipation thinking about seeing Snow.

"Patty," Dr. Rose said, "during our time at the hospital and while we are in sessions, we will need to refer to you as Martha. This will be most important during our work with Snow."

"Oh, yes, of course, I understand. So, past these gates, I'll be Martha, agreed?" she said as Dr. Rose drove past the gate and into the hospital compound.

Martha turned toward Dr. Rose. "Dr. Rose," she said, "I knew if I could get her here within these walls that you would protect and help her."

Dr. Rose reached over and patted Martha's hand. "Dr. Sunn has done so much work with Snow. He brought her out from a catatonic state; her first year with us, she did not speak. We only knew her name because it was in her coat."

Martha's mind raced back, and she was sitting, holding her Toscana coat, sewing Snow DuTro on the label. A sudden feeling of panic and hopelessness engulfed her. She became nauseated and needed to fight off the feeling to stay present.

Dr. Rose noticed that Martha seemed unsteady and asked her," Are you okay?"

"Yes, I'm fine, Dr. Rose, I just felt a little dizzy," she explained.

Chapter Seventeen

Therapy Begins

Once in the hospital, Dr. Rose led Martha to his office and asked her to have a seat and wait until Dr. Sunn could arrive.

Dr. Sunn suddenly came through the door, breathing heavily from rushing in from the parking lot. Together, Dr. Rose and Dr. Sunn walked the hallway to Snow's room.

"Good morning, Aunty Kay. How did you sleep, and did you have your breakfast as yet?" asked Dr. Sunn.

"Yes, to both questions," Aunty Kay replied.

"Well, we want to hold a family session with you," informed Dr. Rose.

"With me and who else?" demanded Aunty Kay. Not waiting for a reply, she said, "Oh no, are you talking about those strange old people? I don't know them, they are not my family."

Dr. Sunn said, "No, we are not talking about them, Aunty Kay. I'm talking about Martha, she is here."

"What are you talking about?" demanded Aunty Kay. "She is with the father, and he will never allow her outside of the house."

"Well, Aunty Kay," said Dr. Sunn, "she is here waiting to see Snow now."

The good doctors opened the door to the study. Then they asked Aunty Kay to have a seat next to Martha. Dr. Rose excused himself by saying, "I'm going to give Jack and Anna a call. Dr. Sunn, will you please run the session?"

Martha stared at Snow until finally she found her words, "Snow, I was afraid I might never see you again. I'm glad the cabby found his way here with you and that you are safe."

Aunty Kay smiled, then said," I know you, you are the mother. You have never been able to keep Snow safe, and I'm sure that you will not now. I expect the father to come through that door and take you and me back to the house where we belong."

Dr. Sunn interjected, "Martha, this is Aunty Kay. She is an alter personality of Snow's. She is a separate entity. She immersed to protect and control because the trauma was so disturbing to Snow's psyche, and things were uncontrollable."

"Aunty Kay, we need your help. Snow has suffered so much, can you help us, please?" pleaded Dr. Sunn.

Aunty Kay just sat on the couch, gazing at the ceiling.

"Martha, is there anything you can say or do, to reach Snow?" Dr. Sunn questioned. "Snow is in there somewhere. She is still conscious, and I believe she can hear you, even if Aunty Kay does not want to help us right now."

"Snow, I hope you can hear me. It's me, your mother. Remember when he allowed us to have time together. I can remember, can you? Remember playing London Bridge," Martha began to sing," London Bridge is falling down, falling down..."

Aunty Kay nearly slipped off the couch onto the floor. She was visibly shaken, and in a weak voice, she said, "I need to know that Snow will be safe before I agree to help."

"Okay, how can we assure you of that. What do you need from us?" asked Dr. Sunn.

"I need proof, but for now, may I please go back to my room?" Aunty Kay requested.

"Sure, of course, I'll call Bob, and he can escort you back there," Dr. Sunn assured her.

After Aunty Kay left the office, Martha inquired, "Was that good?"

"Yes, yes," replied Dr. Sunn. "I think you started to break through with London Bridge. Snow can hear us. We will hold sessions daily, and we will break in."

"And how are you doing with all of this?" asked Dr. Sunn.

"I'm okay, Dr. Sunn," she told him.

Dr. Sunn interrupted, "Please, call me Ray."

"Oh, okay, Ray, I am having so many different thoughts and feelings. But mostly I feel alive and free. I have dreamed about this day for so long, and I knew one day I would be free. Knowing that gave me the motivation and the strength I needed to fight, and here I am! And I will fight to get Snow back, too."

"That's powerful. You are an amazing person. You have survived, and you are resilient," Ray told her.

"Ray, does Snow remember what she has been through?" she asked.

"Martha, she can remember some things, but the alter personalities hold memories. Aunty Kay is still protecting her," he explained.

"That's scary to me," said Martha.

"Why? Please explain more," asked Dr. Sunn.

"Ray, I lived in terror with horrible things inflicted on me by Ali. But what continues to be so hard for me about those times is what I cannot remember. There were times that Ali injected me with one of his many concoctions and then afterward I would see his face, but then things blurred together, then darkness until I awoke alone and in pain. I think not knowing seems even more threatening to me than what I can remember."

"She will remember once the alters are gone, Martha," Ray explained. "I feel that you could benefit from therapy. You need to process the trauma. I believe you have symptoms of PTSD. We have a very good female therapist on staff. She specializes in trauma-based treatment. I'm sure you will like her."

"Okay, Ray, set me up for tomorrow," she agreed. "I will be happy to meet with her. I do want help with all of this."

Dr. Sunn smiled, quickly interjecting, "And of course, client privilege applies."

Dr. Rose walked in. "How did things go?"

"I thought very well," said Dr. Sunn.

"Martha, your father has arranged a meeting at your home with your family attorney," Dr. Rose told her.

"Great, I'm ready," she said. "Will you please give me a ride back home?"

"Yes," he agreed. "Let me gather up the letter and the other evidence for you to give to O'Reilly."

"Patty, as a family friend and your doctor, I plan to see you through this, and I will support you and your family in every way possible. If you need anything, do not hesitate, just ask. By the way, I know Tim O'Reilly, he's a great guy and a good attorney. You're in good hands."

Jack arranged a secret meeting, with his brother and his best friends. The meeting took place outside as it was a beautiful day. Anna set up a luncheon in the garden area, knowing that Patty would benefit from this warm sunny day with plenty of fresh air and sunshine. The men at the table agreed to aid and protect Patty. They developed their plan within three hours from the time they sat down together as collaborators. Homeland security had placed Ali on the no-fly list. They had identified him and his brother Badeel as terrorist. The FBI used the information which Attorney O'Reilly handed over to them to find the hidden safe room and gain entry. They collected DNA samples and other physical evidence to establish that both Martha and Ali had been in the room recently. The general belief was that Ali had killed Martha as he had admitted to on his own phone to Badeel. They believed that he then followed Badeel's instructions and disposed of her body. The men devised shifts, so Patty was always under the watchful eyes of men who would give their own lives for her protection.

The DuTro's arranged to have a memorial service for Martha to say a final good bye. Patty insisted that Anna take a video, so she could watch it later.

"Mom, I want to put Martha to rest in my mind, and it's also a way for me to say good-bye to some old friends," she said. Patty knew she would never be able to see some of the people she cared about face-to-face ever again.

Patty watched the video and mourned her past life as Martha DuTro and completely assumed the identity as Patricia Parsi. Patty was then completely focused on bringing Snow back into her life. So, Patty would meet with Ray first for a family session with Aunty Kay and then Patty would meet with her own therapist daily.

Patty instantly liked her therapist, Dina, from the first session and found that she was able to open up comfortably to her. They not only explored what currently was going on in family sessions, but explored the cause, which was Ali, and her captive years. Patty and her therapist looked in depth at the anguish and the suffering she had endured during those years.

"It was not just the abuse I endured," she explained, "but being forced to live within separate rooms, alone. I had my room, which was large enough, then there was a smaller area that had a table and chair where I could eat. There was also a window that I could see out of, but no one could see me. It was like I was invisible to the world. I was still alive but felt dead in what was truly a gilded cage with beautiful expensive things. I was one of those things, just merely another possession. I was so lonely."

"Patty, that is a dark place, a lonely place in your life, and the fact that you did not receive validation increased your suffering," said Dina.

"The invalidation was breaking me," she continued. "Just to exist for someone else's pleasure and to be so badly used just for the sick and twisted purpose of gratification from such an immoral being. I would ask and plead for mercy, for freedom for myself and Snow. But even in trying to find mercy, I had to use caution. The response from Ali was normally, 'It's the will of Allah to kill or force infidels into submission,' and then I would most likely get an injection that would render me incapable, powerless, to intervene for myself or Snow."

"Patty, you are so resilient and strong, do you think you can go there and acknowledge this about yourself?" she asked.

"Yes, I think I can," she replied.

"Okay, while you are in that place, validate yourself for not being able to move past your captive's control and cruelty," she told her.

"Yes, I understand that," replied a softly sobbing Patty.

"Patty, how to you feel about the therapy so far?" Dina asked.

"I think the sessions are good," she assured her. "I can tell because I'm starting to feel normal again."

"Good, then it is time we collaborate on your goals. What have you been thinking about?" asked Dina.

"Well, I guess I need to have a talk with Dr. Sunn and let him know that I have feelings for him. I need to get my driving license, and I need to find a new home," said Patty.

"Oh, so you have feelings for Dr. Sunn?" Dina asked.

Patty just smiled, blushing a little.

"Those sound like achievable goals to me. You have met unwritten goals already. Exploring past events leads to exposure of them," she went on. "Patty, you are moving beyond victimhood to empowerment. As you move outside of your pain and find validation, you will heal. Okay, Patty, that was a hard session, pick your song to end the session."

Patty had already decided what song she would pick when her therapist asked her, as she always did, to end the individual session with listening to a song. Patty picked 'Sunny,' by Bobby Hebb.

Things was also improving in family session. Aunty Kay had moved to a softer, more compassionate view of Martha, and she did acknowledge during her last session that Snow may actually be safe with her mother. Patty remembered what Aunty Kay told Dr. Sunn at the last session, "I trust you, Dr. Sunn, if you say she is safe, I believe it."

Each family session ended with Patty singing London Bridge. Patty felt in her heart that Snow was listening in her white wonderland. So did Dr. Sunn, he was sure breakthrough was coming.

Patty's days were spent at the hospital. She had become immersed in computers and in all the new and latest technology that had developed since her abduction. She was becoming famous at the center, and she took advantage of the hospital's perks: the pool, the cafeteria, the recreation area, the gardens, the computer lab, and of course, the salon.

Patty had arrived extra early one day, so she could observe Snow without Aunty Kay's awareness. After sitting with staff and observing her through the one-sided window, she found that she had some extra time, so she decided to check out the salon. She was greeted by a stylish, upbeat, little blond-haired woman. "Hello, have you been to the salon before?" she asked.

"No, this is my first time," Patty replied.

"Well then, what are you thinking about, hair, nails, maybe a pedicure?" she asked.

"Wow, can I really have a pedicure?" she asked with an air of excitement as she had not had this type of attention in such a long time.

"Yes, these services are for our clients," she told her. "We want them to take full advantage of them to enjoy being pampered."

"Pick out a color and then come have a seat. My name is Tallulah," she said as she led her to the pedicure chair. "Thinking about doing your hair today, too?"

"Maybe," she replied. "Haven't really decided yet."

"See if you can find something you like in one of these magazines," Tallulah said as she handed Patty a bunch of magazines to look at. Patty walked out of the salon three hours later, looking and feeling quite different with her hair and nails done.

"Hello, Ray," Patty said as she came into his office.

Ray was taken back by Patty's new look. He felt heat in his face rise as he thought about what he should say, then he reconsidered and said nothing.

He felt relieved when Patty asked, "How's my girl?"

Ray thought to himself, Good, I can handle talking about Snow, common ground, but Patty is really a beauty! His thought was interrupted when he heard himself say, "She was enjoying her breakfast, especially the donuts when I last saw her this morning." Ray bent over and hit the buzzer, asking that Snow be brought to the office.

Chapter Eighteen

Awakenings

Bob the orderly opened the door for Snow, but it was still Aunty Kay that walked in and flopped herself down on the couch. Ray began the session by acknowledging the progress from the last session.

"Aunty Kay, you stated that you feel Snow is safe, so we need to move on. So, who do you feel we need to talk to first."

"No, Dr. Sunn, not yet."

"Yes, Aunty Kay, it is time I believe, and I think we should move on promptly," interjected Dr. Sunn.

Patty sat still, hopeful that the therapy was working.

Dr. Sunn walked around the room and said, "Okay, next step. I have this vast blank canvas. I would like to meet with each of the alter personalities and let them each express themselves and their identity."

"Aunty Kay, tell Baby Girl we need her for the session," insisted Dr. Sunn.

"I don't think it is time. You might lose Snow forever, I'm losing control myself. I cannot keep everyone safe!"

"Okay, then trust me, I'm your doctor."

After a few seconds of silence, Aunty Kay gave out a groan, but she agreed, "Yes. You are the doctor, and you are our doctor. Alright, Dr. Sunn, l will ask Baby Girl to attend the session."

Dr. Sunn nodded his head toward Patty. Patty watched as Aunty Kay closed her eyes. Her eyes began to move rapidly under her eye lids.

"Hello, Dr. Sunn," said a childlike voice with a noticeable speech defect.

"Hello, Baby Girl," replied, Dr. Sunn. "Where have you been?"

"Dr. Sunn, Aunty Kay locked us all in the safe room, no one could come to the light."

Then Martha spoke up, "What is going on?"

"Baby Girl, please introduce yourself to Martha."

"Hello, I know you!" said Baby Girl, "you are the mother. I lived in the house with you and the father."

"We believed that Baby Girl emerged when Badeel raped Snow as a child," interjected Dr. Sunn.

Baby Girl continued, "That is true. Snow did not feel what the bad man did. I was there for Snow."

Martha started to cry. "Can I give you a hug?"

"Yes, Mommy," replied Baby Girl. Tears ran down Patty's face as she hugged Baby Girl.

The session was powerful. Baby Girl painted her three dolls on the canvas. After the session, Dr. Sunn pointed out, "Baby Girl called you mommy, Martha."

It took another session before Baby Girl was gone. "Martha, Baby Girl is gone and moved on just as Bud had done. Those horrifying memories she held locked away from Snow are now Snow's memories. Bud was the first alter to submerged and leave, now Baby Girl is gone," assured Dr. Sunn.

"Who is Bud?" Martha questioned Dr. Sunn.

"He was a part of Snow's psychic that expressed humor during the times when laughter was unthinkable for her. Bud left during an early group therapy session," explained Dr. Sunn.

Then Martha asked him, "But how can you be sure he is gone?"

Dr. Sunn smiled, feeling just a little uneasy and told her, "He is gone. We have not heard from him since he left a couple months ago."

During the next session, Aunty Kay asked Louie to attend. Louie painted a muscle arm with a clinched fist and a cloud with lightning bolts. Louie told Martha how he fought for Snow, he told her about the first time he emerged when the father had become so angry with Snow and lost his temper. Louie reconnected and then said his good byes. The three sat in silence, inspecting the painting. After several minutes had past, they all agreed that the painting was taking shape. The daily sessions continued as Martha and Snow were making progress. Jack and Anna also sat in during some of the sessions. They also began to heal.

* * * * *

Ray sat at his desk alone. He was expecting Patty, but she was running late for the session. Just then, Nurse Vickie told Ray, "Patty is on the phone."

Ray picked up the phone, and Patty explained that Jack was in a meeting with a realtor and that he was unable to get away, so she was calling to cancel the session. Then a light came on as Ray stood with the phone in his hand, "She doesn't know how to drive, she can't drive. Of course! When could she have learned?" Ray cleared his voice, then said, "I'll be there in about ten minutes, just wait for me."

Ray pulled up and walked up to the front door. Patty was standing there waiting. "This is so nice of you to pick me up and give me a ride."

"I'm not giving you a ride," Ray told her.

"What, then why are you here?" she asked.

"You are going to drive! Today, you will learn, let's go," He told her.

Patty held back with a rush of excitement, "Really, I did drive a little before my abduction. Let's go. I'll race you to the car!"

Laughs and jokes were the course for the day. Therapy sessions were postponed as the focus was on Ray teaching Patty how to drive again. After the lesson, Ray took Patty to a quaint little restaurant not far from the St. Louis Arch.

"What a great day!" Patty exclaimed. "I knew life would be good again. And I knew I would find a man like my father; kind, understanding, and safe."

"That is such a nice thing to say. I thank you for saying those things to me." said Ray. "Patty, do you remember when I first asked you to call me Ray and not Dr. Sunn?"

"Yes, I do remember that," she replied.

"I didn't want to be your doctor or for you to call me your doctor because I noticed that I had feelings toward you. I know this is a very hard time for you. All of your energy and focus needs to be on getting healthy. I just had to let you know how I feel, I had to say those words to you while I had enough courage," Ray told her.

"It's okay Ray, I feel it, too," she told him. "But I'm not good now, I'm truly broken. One day I'll be whole and healthy. I will let you know, Ray, when that day comes."

"Good, now let's agree to use a therapy technique and shelve this conversation and our feelings. Let's put them up on the shelve, and one day we will get them down again and talk about it then," said Ray softly.

"Yes, Ray, I agree," she told him. "One day after Snow's therapy is completed and she is also whole." Patty gave Ray a light kiss on his lip and asked, "Will you take me home now?"

The next morning, Patty woke up knowing what direction her life was going in. Patty was so excited, she ran down the stairs for breakfast, asking, "So, what did the realtor say, is he going to help us?"

"Well, let us eat and talk," said Jack.

"Yeah! I'm so happy that I can have breakfast with you both. I thank GOD every day."

"So do we!" Anna said.

"Okay, where are we now with the move? It's too risky to stay in this town much longer. I saw Sue the other day coming out of the grocery store, she took a double take at me. I thought she might had recognized me, but she kept on walking away in the other direction. If we stay here, it's only a matter of time before someone identifies me as Martha DuTro."

"Your mother and I have talked about that also, and we know we have to do something soon, but it's a matter of timing. How is Snow? We don't want to rush her or move her until she has recovered. We are so blessed to have you home, and we know that Snow is getting better. Life is good again, and it keeps getting better day by day," said Jack.

"You're right, Dad, I think that we need to stay together, too, and when it's time, we move together," said Patty, looking up at her parents. She went on to say, "I've been looking at hotel properties in Miami on the beach. I want to live with culture and be surrounded by people. If you're a marked duck, it's best if you are surrounded by ducks. In Miami, we would just blend in. Mom, you have said ever since I can remember that you wanted to retire in Florida. And Father, you been talking about doing some big fishing."

"And what about you, Patty?" asked Jack, "what do you want?"

"First, I want to live with my family," she replied. "I want to have people that love me and people I love around me every day. I want to live and own a fabulous, glamorous, fascinating place."

"Patty, that sounds exciting," said her mom.

"I know, Mom, and it can happen. I also would like to use my talents to entertain people," Patty went on. "When I play and sing, I am never at that place of misery. Entertaining people moves me on past my suffering. I can make people happy by entertaining them, they can forget their cares and worries. And I know how all of this can happen. We can invest in a family business, our own hotel. I plan on being the opening act in our family owned hotel. Mom, I know that hospitality is your calling and mine is entertaining. Dad, you are a great business man. I have it all planned out in my mind. I always knew that entertaining others would be my career. I'm really good at it, I bless people with it, and I love it!"

Jack and Anna sat smiling and listening intensely.

"We will also hold auditions for local talents. We will book local artists. It will be good for the hotel and for the people in the area. We can give chances to people that might not have one otherwise, a chance to show off their talents. We will find hidden talents and give people a chance to shine."

"So, what will we call this fabulous hotel?" asked her mom.

"Well, Mom, how about Starlights, Arabian Night Escape."

"It's catchy, might bring in a lot of tourist, lovers, honeymooners, and people just looking for an adventure," Jack agreed.

"If I can sing and play the piano, that will be part of my life mission. Then if I can have exceptional accommodations for people, I will feel another life mission has been achieved. You know, Mom, maybe we can the help the less fortunate, too," said Patty.

"I like it," said Anna, nodding her head.

"As a captive that was beaten, mistreated, and shut in, I realized that there were other hurting Americans, too. Hungry, cold, and suffering. I want to reach out and say, 'I understand.' And if I can find a realistic approach to help the homeless, abused, and forgotten, I know God will be proud of me. HE told me I would live and that my life would be more abundant. So, I choose to live like that and be a blessing to others."

"Okay, let's put these plans into action. I already have a gifted, committed realtor. Phase one will be to find and purchase the 'Starlights Arabian Night Escape.' The letters stand for SANE, so we will refer to our hotel as SANE. It will be our little joke," Jack said with a chuckle. "Anna, we are going to find that hotel. Get ready, we are going to take off and go to Miami this week. Patty, you concentrate on helping our Snow get better and get your driving license."

Anna broke in," Yes, Daddy, we are going to the DMV in St. Charles county and then to the hospital for our family session today."

When Anna and Patty arrived at the hospital, Snow was in the office and her entity Aunty Kay was in full control.

"No, no, no, it is too soon for Martha and Dawn to talk. Dr. Sunn, you will suspend Snow forever in her safe place, the frozen domicile, if you continue with this."

"Okay, calm down, Aunty Kay! Let's discuss this and explore the options," Dr. Sunn said as he saw Anna and Patty standing by the door. "Come on in, both of you. Aunty Kay is feeling threatened."

"No, I'm not, as I do now and have always felt, my concern is for Snow! Dawn keeps the ugliest truth about the father within herself, away from Snow."

Anna interjected, "Please go on, Aunty Kay, we all want to protect and help Snow recover."

"Okay, please listen to me, this is dangerous," she continued. "Dawn has compartmentalized, and as a result, Snow sees the father in a catalogic type. She has memories of the mother being sick and insane. She has memories of the father and of her Aunt Joy as being caregivers, not prisoner guards."

"Okay, I get it. We all do," said Martha. "We need to be cautious."

"Yes," said Dr. Sunn. "But I have done the hard work and so has Snow. She had to break through her own chaotic state. She fought hard and it was painful for her to allow Bud, the first alter personality, to leave. Bud submerged and left only through Snow's desire to change. She is strong!"

Peering at Aunty Kay, Dr. Sunn said, "Aunty Kay, you are aware of this, and to be honest, you fought to shut her down and to keep the disassociation in full force. Aunty Kay, you must let go. Martha is here, now and present, the past is gone. We need to look at the past here in this safe, clinical setting. Aunty Kay, Snow's very existence and healing is entwined with Martha. Once Snow is whole again, Martha can heal, and Snow's family will support her and keep her safe. You have done your job, now please, let us talk to Dawn," Dr. Sunn pleaded with his voice and eyes.

"Oh, Lordy me!" came a unique voice with a southern drawl. It was Dawn.

"Hello, Dawn. How are you?" asked Dr. Sunn. "Let me introduce you to Anna, Snow's grandmother. And you know Martha."

"Martha, I'm just so happy to see you, you look so beautiful and happy," Dawn said as she grabbed Martha as tears ran down her face. Martha also began to cry. She was holding her daughter in her arms, and they were crying together, tears of joy. Anna also felt tears running down her cheeks. She stole a glance at Dr. Sunn, and she could see his tears also. After a few minutes, everyone reigned in their emotions.

"Let's continue," said, Dr. Sunn. "Dawn, what do you think about the painting we have been working on?" Dr. Sunn pointed out what Baby Girl had painted and what Louie had painted.

"Oh, I can see this needs a southern woman's touch," she exclaimed as she examined the painting.

Dawn turned to Martha. "Martha, the first time I emerged was when Snow had snuck into your room. She was giggling and was going to slip into your bed and snuggle up with you. Ali had already drugged you that night. He came into the room. I can still remember the smell, it was the smell of alcohol. Anyway, Snow slipped down quietly and hid under the bed. She heard as Ali hit you. She heard you scream and then I took over. I saw what he did to you. I saw as he bit into your flesh. I witnessed him rape and torture you. Do you remember that night, Martha?"

"Yes, Ali was especially brutal to me that night, Snow," said Martha.

"No, Snow is not here, it's me, Dawn!" she corrected her.

Martha went on, "Okay, Dawn, I remember that night and other nights like that. And I remember those times through pain, humiliation, and shame. And all through a maze of drugs. Worse than remembering is when I can't remember. I might remember lying in bed, then waking

SNOW AT THE DOME

up in pain. Sometimes I was bloody and unable to walk steady. Sometimes, like that night, I have glimpses of Snow's little face, hiding."

Dawn asked her, "And you are sure you want Snow to have these memories?"

Dr. Sunn interjected, "Martha, I know it feels to you like a piece of your life is missing because you cannot remember exactly what was done to you. And that probably is a good thing, but your subconscious does remember. Dawn holds many incidents of Ali hurting you, Martha. Dawn has seen some horrific events, but as you say, the worst thing is not remembering. It's that void. Knowing something evil and ugly is hiding within your own mind but not being able to access it."

Dawn went on, "I have witnessed Ali being brutal to Martha four times. This was the first time. The second time was when Snow hid in Martha's bathroom. The third time was when Badeel took Snow as his child bride, and the fourth time was about a month before the planned escape."

"Martha, I do not mean to diminish the horrible torture you endured, but I'm glad to know that there was a limit to what Snow was exposed to, what she saw, and witnessed."

Then, Dr. Sunn took a deep breath and turned his attention toward Anna. "Anna, are you okay? And what are you feeling hearing this disclosure?"

"Yes, I just was taken back for a moment." Red faced, Anna continued, "I'm infuriated that there was an animal who so mistreated my baby, my little girl! Martha, I want you to know, I'm also proud to be your mom because you have been so strong. You fought for yourself and for your daughter, and I know we will stand together and heal from this, all of us," Dawn and Martha both grabbed Anna and gave her hugs.

"Dawn, are you ready to complete your part of the painting?" Dr. Sunn now asked.

"Yes, Dr. Sunn, and I am ready to entrust Snow with my secrets. Once I'm gone, she will remember, but facing that pain will lead to more healing." Dawn began to paint. She added beautiful colors, lipstick, a high heel shoe, and a glitter clutch purse.

"Before I leave, I do have something significant to say to you all. Snow will need to see males in positive roles being strong, loving, supportive, and showing strength through gentleness," added Dawn.

"Don't worry, Dawn, her grandfather, Jack, is a man like that and so is Dr. Sunn," Martha said as an affirmation.

The session ended with Dawn closing her eyes, submerging into the subconscious. Then Aunty Kay was back. As the established routine, Patty sang London Bridge. Snow had a smile on her face, and Aunty Kay said she felt exhausted and needed to go to her room.

"Dr. Sunn, will you let Dina know that I'm really overwhelmed, and I do not feel like I can endure an individual session today?"

"Of course," he replied. "You two take off and go shopping. Have some fun!"

"Well, how about going to the DMV?" asked Martha. "That's differential attention, right, Dr. Sunn? And I need to put my focus on something."

"Sounds good," Dr. Sunn said as he closed Snow's file.

• • • • •

Patty and Anna did go to the DMV, using her new ID as Patti DuTro since the adoption papers had been filed. Patty passed her test, then they went shopping, and they enjoyed a great barbecue sandwich.

Jack was waiting at home with good news. The realtor had found a hotel in Miami on South Beach. "Are you ready for a trip to Miami?" he asked. "Our realtor said we need to move quickly if we want to secure the property."

"How soon can we leave, Jack?" Anna asked.

"I can book our tickets for Saturday," he said.

"Book the tickets, Dad," answered Anna.

Patty called her therapist, Dina, and asked if she could see her prior to the next scheduled family session. Dina agreed. Patty's therapist was seated in her therapy chair when Patty arrived the next morning.

"Come on in, Patty, and have a seat," she told her.

"Good, thank you," Patty started. "I need to talk to you before I have another family session. The last session with Dr. Sunn was so revealing for me, sometimes secrets need to be kept from family members for their own good. I saw how destructive disclosing the abuse was for my poor mother."

"I see, go on, Patty," Dina said.

"When Dawn described how Ali had hurt me, my mother said it knocked the breath out of her. The abuse from Ali was so horrific that my little Snow split into different entities because she was not able to face what she saw Ali do to me. This must end. I cannot let Ali hurt anyone else. I have decided not to disclose any more about what I suffered during my captive years in front of my family."

"If you decide to take that position, it might be difficult," Dina cautioned.

"This is not the first time I decided to guard my response and disclosures," Patty went on. "I lived a lie for 13 years for Snow's sake. I had to pretend and help Ali in his falsehood that I was insane and he was the caring father. As long as Snow believed the mirage, she was safe. But it sickened me. Even after Snow got away, I still had to pretend, I sat there as a captive for another three years. Just waiting for Snow to bring the authorities or to hear a knock on the door. I often was fearful that Snow did not make it and that she had died from the injection, but I had to believe she was alive, so I waited."

"No person should have to go through what you endured. I know it was horrendous, you were in such a grave situation for so many years," said Dina.

"Now I'm on the other side of that time," Patty continued. "I survived and am now reunited with my parents and Snow. I feel that talking about the abuse and letting them see how I suffered makes the people I love victims and revictimizes me. So, I will stay empowered by only talking to you about the torture and abuse I have suffered." Patty then gave out a loud breath and looked toward her therapist.

Dina told her, "Patty, that is your decision. Disclosing in a family session can inflict pain on members in your family, and I agree with you about how painful it must be for your loved ones. The past cannot be changed, and if you disclose here and process the trauma in individual therapy, you're good. So, how are your goals coming?"

"I have found a hotel, I have my driving license, and I did let Dr. Sunn know I have feelings for him," she told her.

"Patty, you are making progress. You have met the goals you established for yourself. Why do you think you can stay so strong and resilient?" Dina questioned her.

"Am I?" asked Patty.

"Yes, you are strong," replied her therapist.

"I was raised in a Christian home. I was my dad's little princess like most little girls. I was my mom's little helper, and I was Kenneth's little sister. I was loved and valued by my family. It's interesting when I think about it but Kenny, my oldest brother, laid down the blue print. Respect Mom and Dad, get good grades, be friendly, help others, and love music. And when my brother was killed in combat, I hurt deep in my heart, the pain was intense, and I saw how his death hurt my parents. But somehow the death of my brother made me stronger. I guess the answer to your question is that I was loved."

Dina agreed. "Yes, I can see that. Stay strong and know that you can have any type of life you want. We each have the power to bring change in our lives. So, what song have you picked out for this week?"

"Singing in the Rain," Patty said with a smile. They ended the session listening to music.

Patty felt like a weight had been taken off her shoulders. She had a bounce to her walk as she walked to Dr. Sunn's office.

"Good morning, Patty," greeted Dr. Sunn. "Are you ready for this session? We must confront Aunty Kay, so Hope can submerge."

"Dr. Sunn, I want my daughter back," Patty told him. "This is the last part of my nightmare. I won't be able to move on until it is ended."

"Good, Aunty Kay is on her way," Dr. Sunn told her.

The session began with Aunty Kay warning Dr. Sunn, "You are pushing too hard. You might lose Snow forever if you continue."

"Yes, yes, Aunty Kay, we acknowledge all of your concerns for Snow," he assured her. "And as I have voiced in the past and as I remind you now, I'm Snow's doctor, and I need you to trust me. Please call Hope, we want her to attend this session."

Aunty Kay sat with her arms crossed and a scowl on her face. Then her face seemed to lighten and then there was the smile. That big, beautiful, bright smile that belonged to Hope.

"I told you I would see you again, Dr. Sunn," said Hope.

"Hello, Hope, we need you to help us," he told her. "Can you tell us what we need to do now to help Snow?"

"Of course, that is why I'm here," she assured him.

"Hello, Hope."

"Hello, Martha. The last time I was able to help you was three years ago. I had to fight Aunty Kay." Hope remembered that day. "She tried to stop me! I even had to wrestle Louie."

"What day are you talking about?" asked Martha.

"Martha, it was the day you asked Snow to take the note to school for Mr. Graham. Snow was too scared, and she didn't trust you. So, I took over. It was me that took the note to Mr. Graham. Do you remember?" Hope asked.

"Yes, yes, I remember being nervous, I thought Snow might refuse out of fear for Ali. But when I asked, she said yes and smiled," Martha recalled.

"So, you do remember. That was me!" Hope said.

"Can I give you a hug, Hope, and thank you for taking my note to Mr. Graham? It was your courage that opened the door to freedom," said Martha.

"Now I have something important to tell you both," Hope said. "Snow is trying to find her way out of the frozen land. She can hear you when you talk, and when you sing, she also remembers. We are all just fragmented parts of Snow. Snow does have courage and hope. Dr. Sunn, I am ready to leave." Hope walked over to the painting and began to paint. She added a dove and beautiful gold colors to the painting. She turned and smiled, "Sing, Martha, sing London Bridge." And then she was gone.

Aunty Kay stood in front of the painting for the first time. Then she began to paint orange blossoms and beautiful pink flowers. "Dr. Sunn, I do trust you and Martha. I can see how you protect Snow. You put Snow before yourself, and you're a good mother, Martha."

Martha sat singing the chorus of London Bridge as Aunty Kay continue to paint. Aunty Kay was engrossed in the painting. She painted beautiful bright colors and added butterflies.

Martha stopped her singing and gently said, "Snow, I hope you can hear me. I feel I need to tell you why I named you Snow. When I first looked at your beautiful little face and felt your soft skin, I felt as if your presence covered up the hard, ugly things in that house. Your birth was like fresh fallen snow. When I was a kid in Missouri, I would get so excited about the last snow in March. Because I knew the fresh fallen snow would bring life to the tulips that were under the cold, hard ground. It never failed, all I had to do was to wait and watch for the day that the little flowers would push through the snow. The last snow fall was what was needed to bring about new life and growth. That is why I named you Snow."

Suddenly, Snow stopped painting and began to sing London Bridge.

"Snow, did you find your way out?"

"Dr. Sunn, what happened? I was talking to you and then I began to fall."

"Snow, please put the brush down and turn around," asked Dr. Sunn.

Snow turned around slowly, and as she turned, Martha suddenly was in front of her. "Mom, Mom!" she cried out as she reached out to her mother and crumpled in her arms.

Dr. Sunn, Patty, and Snow continued with the family session as the only three entities in the room finally. They sat together, admiring the beautiful unique painting. Snow smiled when she saw that there was a big pizza pie in the center of the painting.

Snow continued to have individual sessions with Dr. Sunn. Her recovery was remarkably fast after the break through. She went home with Patty for an overnight visit the first week. Then Snow started to go home for the weekend. Within a month, she moved home with Patty and her grandparents. Snow continued to be seen by Dr. Sunn in his office weekly, then monthly, then bi-monthly, and then she did not need to see him at all. Patty kept Dr. Sunn informed on Snow's progress and on the progress of purchasing and moving into the hotel. Each call that came in from Patty was like a flurry of excitement. Patty described trips to Miami and how her mom and Snow were so immersed in the remodeling and renovation of the hotel.

Then one day, Dr. Sunn stood in his office and remembered his former client, Snow, and her beautiful mother and hoped that they were doing fine. It would be six years before Ray would see them again.

Chapter Nineteen

The Visitor

Patty came rushing into the hotel lobby running up to the front desk. "George, is my father in his office?" she asked excitedly.

"Yes, Ms. Patty," he replied, "but he is interviewing for the manager position."

"Oh, okay, thanks, George. Will you tell him I need to talk to him and that I'll be in my office."

Patty rushed into her office and started going through the planner on her desk. The phone rang. "Hello, yes, we are expecting the center to open this Monday. The official ceremony is tomorrow at 4pm. Yes, okay. Snow DuTro is our contact, you can set it up with her. She would be happy to give you an interview."

Jack gave a quick knock on Patty's door and then stuck his head in. Patty waved him in.

"Are you busy?"

"No, not really, just waiting for you," Jack told her.

"That was channel four news. They want to cover the opening of the community center. It's going to be televised, so of course I gave them Snow's name as the contact. Dad, how did the interview go with Dalir?"

"Great, I think. I also think that we have found our new manager to replace our Lilly if anyone could ever replace her. I plan on calling Dalir Monday to make a verbal offer for the position and to give her the details of her annual salary. I believe she will take our offer. She will have a very nice package from us. It will take a while to fully train her, but I really like her," Jack told Patty.

"Oh, Dad, so much is going on. What a time for Lilly to resign."

"I know, but it's going to be alright, you'll see. George took up most of the slack. We have six suites reserved for our guest. The meals are planned and even the main table seating chart is done. Now you, my girl, just need to practice your song and come across strong. Patty, I know we have been so busy the last few months. I haven't made the time to check in to see how you're doing. I suppose I knew you did not need my help."

"And just what gave you that idea?" she asked.

"The way you got this hotel up and running and turned it into the most desired place to stay on the strip. And the fact that you are the attraction to this grand hotel. People pack in on the weekends just to see and hear your act," he told her.

"Dad, the success of the hotel is from the efforts of all of us, you, Mom, and Snow. And I'm a born entertainer, and I love it. I knew during my captive years that once I had my chance, I would live this type of life. I hoped one day I would have the opportunity to invite people in. To excite people! And that I would never be hidden again, I would be seen and applauded. You and Mom stepped in to make this all a reality. The way you took over the hiring of the staff, the permits, the attorneys, you worked hard, Father. And the way mom and Snow went to work on the hotel design. Dad, it was us working together as a family, as a team! All of our hard work led to our successes."

"Patty, we have endured and pulled together. That is why we are a successful family."

"And our biggest success is Snow, don't you agree?" she asked. "She really needed us at first, and the way you and Mom were there to support her. Helping her meet with the board, helping her with her papers, and just encouraging her. She is thankful for all the help and support you both gave her. She worked harder than most and overcame a difficult task to get her MSW, then she continued to work hard and meet her requirements to get her licenses. And father, she's a great therapist and she found a good guy in Duane. I'm so proud of her. The odds she overcame. I would like to take some of the credit, but I know I can't. What kind of mother was I, a pitiful captive."

"Stop it, Patty, you are a great mother. Snow wouldn't have survived without you," he assured her.

"Dad, I question that. She is so intelligent. Ray said for her to have fabricated such a complex world with effective alters, she is a genius!"

"Yes, you're right, Patty. I know I have a brilliant, sensitive, beautiful granddaughter that we can all be proud of, and I have a daughter that has conquered injustice, a foreign ideologic. And you came out with a heart to serve and enchant mankind with your gifts."

"Dad, I love you."

"Sometimes I feel that I failed you," he responded. "We taught you to pledge your allegiance to this great country that we are so blessed to live in. But yet, we have a cancer within that is killing our freedoms and our way of life. Our freedoms are being used against us. Since the time of our founding fathers, men have fought for our way of life. We have fought our enemies here and overseas to protect our families and allies from oppression. But now we are accused of being haters because we want to protect our country and its citizens from the foreign hostility within. Although I fought for this country alongside many other brave men and women, plus your brother died for this country, I could not protect you and no one did," a sobbing Jack said, "why wasn't something more done."

"Dad, you and Mom did all you could do, both of you! Dad, have you thought that I could have been taken by an American citizen and held captive, sexually exploited, and maybe even killed! Predators are often neighbors or relatives of their victims."

"Yes, that is true, Patty. But we would be able to obtain some type of justice for you and Snow. An American citizen would be facing life imprisonment or death. This Ali has the support of his country to do what he did, and let's not forget he is emboldened by his beliefs to commit his vile crimes. And now we do not know where this monster is. It's not fair to you or Snow to live with such a threat hanging over you both."

"Dad, we have talked about this before, and we are all aware of this. We choose to forgive and to live without fear. That is the American way, our way."

"Dad, this might not make any sense to you, but I'm thinking about one time when I was little. We had gone downtown to pick up some flowers for Mom's birthday. I saw the pony outside of the dime store. I ran and jumped on it. I remember begging you to let me ride the pony. It was only a quarter. You smiled and put your hands into your pockets, searching for a quarter. Then you started searching all of your pockets, but you didn't have a quarter right then at that time. You had thousands of quarters but not at that time and not that day. The day Ali took me was like that day. If you had known, you would have stopped it. No guilt, Dad, it's toxic. Just know that if you had had a quarter that day, you would have put it in the slot, and I would have ridden the pony. If you had known that a visitor was coming into our country and that he would abduct me someday, you wouldn't had let him in. You would have told the authorities that there is a man arriving, he is coming as a visitor, and he plans to kidnap my 13-year-old daughter. They would have stopped him. You have so much love, but you didn't have the information, so all of your love couldn't start or stop the pony ride or Ali."

Patty and Jack looked at each other with tears in their eyes, quickly recovering their emotions, they both said spontaneously, "Where is Mom?"

"Oh, she is overseeing the kitchen," Jack replied. "Mom loved your idea about opening up the café to the homeless after breakfast has been served in the café. She told me she thoroughly enjoys mingling and talking with people, and she feels that she is making a difference by serving the homeless and as she says," Jack and Patty chimed in together, "those in need!" Then they looked at each other and chuckled.

"Mom told me that for the last few weeks there has been a family of eight that eats breakfast here. She told me as soon as the kitchen closes at 11, they are here. She told me she was able to talk to the mother. Mom said that the woman said she was so grateful. And that she was amazed that a big hotel, like SANE, would actually close their café from 11am to 1pm to let the needy come in and eat for free. To give the poor the food that was left from a fabulous chef's buffet. The woman went on to say her children feel so special and that they love coming here for breakfast. She said that her children are now able to have a healthy breakfast during the summer when school is out. Mom said she told her the children named the breakfast, 'the Free Standing Breakfast.'"

"It was and still is a simple but great idea for us and for the community," Jack said as he took and squeezed Patty's hand.

"Well, Father, I should get going. I want to meet our guests. I'm so excited. Uncle Don and Aunt Louise are coming, attorney Tim, Bob, our favorite realtor Charly, and your old ex-employee, Joe!"

Jack broke in, "And Dr. Sunn!"

Patty made a clearing sound in her throat, "Father, you mean Ray?"

"Well, he has been a life saver for this family. It's been six years since we have seen him, right?" Jack said with a wink.

"Yeah, that's right, and he will be here today!" said a cheerful smiling Patty as she and Jack left the office to go to the lobby.

The guest began to arrive. First, Uncle Don and Aunt Louise walked through the lobby doors, Jack went off with his brother Don and his wife Louise to show them the grounds and their rooms. Patty was talking with George when Anna and Snow came in.

"Oh, good, let's make sure each of our special guest has one of us to welcome them," her words trailed off as she saw Ray walking through the lobby doors.

Snow stood and took a deep breath in her lungs to give her enough breath to loudly yell, "Dr. Sunn, Dr. Sunn!" Snow continued to repeat his name as she ran towards him. She grabbed him and gave him a big hug, not letting him go, she just held onto him for quite some time. Surely, tears of joy ran down Snow's face, and tears also welled up in Patty's eyes. After a few minutes, Patty asked George to make sure that Ray's luggage was attended to. She then turned toward Snow and Ray and then she approached Ray as steady as a person could that felt so elated as she did. She thought to herself, I'm so happy that it's hard not to cry. She then asked Snow and Anna to wait at the registration desk until the rest of the guest arrived.

"Come on with me, Ray," Patty said, grabbing his hand. "I am going to be your personal guide, I want to first show you to your room, then the hotel, then you can see the grounds, and then I especially want you to see the beach!" Patty and Ray gazed at each other, walking hand in hand.

"Patty, this place is amazing, it's breathtaking. Those palm trees are enormous that surround the hotel, and all those large leafy plants, the beautiful flowers, and the exotic birds, so peaceful and beautiful. This hotel itself is just gorgeous. I love the marble, the carpeting, the wall hangings, and those beautiful tropical plants! It is just stunning, all of it. And then there is you. When I arrived and saw you standing there among what looks like paradise, I thought to myself, Eve could not had been more beautiful, and Adam could not had been more moved by her beauty than I am by yours. Patty, you're the most beautiful creature I have ever seen!"

"Ray, that's so romantic, I love it. I'll hide what you just told me deep in my heart and remember it forever."

"Ray, I have kept all your letters. I read them over and over. Especially the first one you wrote me after I had left Missouri. I was so excited when I got your letter. I was even more excited when I read it and saw it was about us and the love we shared. Ray, it's been a long time since we have seen each other face to face but the letters and phone calls have kept us close, and now, you're here with us. I'm beyond happy! Are you sure it has been long enough for Snow to heal? Never mind, we can talk about that later. Come on, let me show you your room."

"Patty, I do have a confession," Ray said with hesitation.

"Well, what is it, Ray?"

"You know how we use the 'other side' in therapy?"

"Yes, Ray, I use that technique you taught us."

"Well, I'm on the other side. I do believe Snow has had more than sufficient time to heal. I do not believe that my presence will trigger her. We have waited long enough. I have waited years. And yet, the facts of how we met and fell in love triggered me. On the long train ride here, and it was a long ride by my design, so I could consider everything. If you had not been kidnapped by that horrible cruel man, I would never had met Snow."

"Ray, I understand, I'm on the other side of Ali, too."

"Patty, let me finish what I need to say. You're such a beautiful, talented, and awesome woman. My intellect tells me that you would not have given me a second look if I hadn't been Snow's therapist. I know I'm just an average man."

"Now, you stop, Ray, and let me finish. Dr. Ray Sunn, you are anything but an average man. You are a gifted therapist, a wise doctor, a compassionate person, and a man who knows how to love. We have forfeited six long years until we could be together, no more! We will not be forlorn any more, nor will we entertain misplaced guilt. I have suffered more than most, and you have waited for me longer than most men. No more!" Once in the room, Patty drew the drapes, displaying the gulf view.

But Ray was not looking at the beach, he was staring at Patty. "Let's take those feelings off the shelf, it's time, it's our time." Ray then knelt before Patty and asked, "Martha, Patty DuTro, will you please marry me and become my wife."

Patty heard the word marry me, and her mind swiftly went back to her past. She remembered how Ali had knelt before her on his knees and how she became furious and how she used that opportunity to gain her freedom. She remembered lifting the heavy metal box over her own head and bringing it down with her full force, hitting him on the head.

Patty looked at Ray, and she again felt flooded with emotion. This time it was love and respect. Patty experienced jubilee in her heart. She visualized herself walking up to her own beating heart. When she looked inside, there was a box locked up tight with a huge chain lock. She took a key and unlocked the box. Then she heard her voice say, "Yes, Ray, I will marry you and be your wife!"

Patty and Ray embraced, then Patty led Ray into the bedroom, where they fell on the vast rattan bed. Hours later, they emerged together and walked the grounds, hand in hand.

"So, Ray, this is the plan," Patty said, breaking into the quietness. "Tomorrow at 4 pm, we open the community center. Then we will come back here for the dinner. I think we should announce our engagement then. After the dinner, we can spend time with Snow to see where she is with us being a couple and the fact that you will be her stepfather. Then it will be time for my performance. I want you to know, Ray, that I will be entertaining everyone, but I'll only be singing to you." The lovers kissed and then retreated back to the rattan bed.

Before dinner that night, Patty left and went to her room to get dressed for dinner. Once she was back in her room alone, she fell on her knees and gave thanks to God for Snow, her parents, and for the love of her life, Ray. Patty got dressed in a light cotton dress, then she arranged her hair in an up rap, put on her gold earrings, bangle bracelets, and her favorite gold necklace. Then, after slipping on her meshed shoes, she walked out to the dining room.

The table was set and prepared for the people that loved her the most and shared her family's deepest secrets. Patty was seated next to Ray. They all ordered and ate a delicious lobster meal. The night was filled with energy and excitement. Patty and Ray found it a difficult task not to keep looking at each other, and everyone at the table noticed. Snow was on the other side of Ray, and on her other side, Duane was seated.

Patty whispered into Ray's ear, "I am sure Snow wants to introduce you to her fiancé, Duane. You will really like him, he is a really great guy, and he loves her so much."

Ray smiled and nodded his head, then said, "Snow, I've heard from your mother that you love working as a therapist?"

"Yes, Dr. Sunn."

"Please, Snow, call me Ray."

"Okay, Ray, but that sounds a little strange."

"You will get used to it, it's exposure. I'm Ray now, no longer your doctor, Snow, and you are not my patient anymore."

"I know," she responded.

"And who is that sitting next to you?" Ray asked.

"Ray, I'm pleased to introduce you to my fiancé, Duane Owens. He is also a psychiatrist."

"Nice to meet you, Duane, I'm Ray."

"Yes, I know. Snow has told me all about you and your work. She has told me everything, and I'm very happy to finally meet you, Ray. We are great together, and I think we make a great team as therapist and psychiatrist."

"Sounds like you're already a team," Ray said as he reached across Snow to shake Duane's hand.

"Hmm, said Snow. It looks like we are not the only new team setting at the table." Snow smiled at Ray. "You and Mom seem like you might be hitching up or something, too?"

"Oh, really good job at observing."

"Everyone can sense the chemistry," she said.

"Well, Snow, if that was so, what do you think? Would we make a good match?"

"Yes, it has always been written that you and Mom were meant for each other. And there is no other person that walks this earth I would rather see her with than you."

"Snow, could you see me as a stepfather?"

"Yes, Ray, and I think that you would be a good father."

Jack was watching the exchange at the table that was taking place between Snow and Ray. He directed his voice toward Ray. "When dinner is over, let's meet on the verandah. I have some excellent cigars."

Ray smiled. "Meet you there," he said as he gave a head nod towards Jack.

Laughter, chattering, and conversation continued to ascend from the close group at the table. Patty was a perfect host, it was easy for her. She not only loved everyone sitting at the table, but that night, she was *in* love, and her lover was seated next to her. Patty had thought at one time during the dinner that she wished it could go on for days but then she remembered that the community center was opening the next day.

Ray broke into her thoughts, "Patty, your father asked me to meet him on the verandah for a cigar."

Patty pointed out the pathway that led to the verandah, "Ray, I'll meet you out on the verandah later, go on then."

Ray enjoyed his walk on the pathway lined with lush tropical plants. The palm trees tops were hustling as the winds blew between their fronds. The air was full of sweet aromas as the beautiful birds of paradise gave off their fragrance. Ray spotted Jack sitting on a white wicker chair.

"Come over here and pull up a chair." Jack asked Ray what type of cocktail would you like to drink.

"Something tropical, I think?" he answered.

Jack ordered two Pina Coladas and handed Ray a cigar. The men sat, preparing to smoke the cigars. "Ray, I just wanted to say how sorry I was when I heard that Peter, Dr. Rose, was unable to come because his wife Tina was suddenly taken ill."

"Yes, he felt bad that he wasn't able to come."

"He is one of the community centers benefactors. You might not be aware that he had intended to make you an offer for the director job of the center? I have an envelope here with the offer and the salary. But that's not the only reason I wanted to talk with you, Ray," Jack said as he exhaled a puff of smoke. "I need to tell you that I, myself, and my family will always be in your debt for what you did for Snow. Peter and I have been friends for many years, and he explained to me that you had to gain Snow's trust in order to help her. He told me that you went into her world of delusion and chaos to bring her out. She is such a beautiful creature, and she has a beautiful soul, we thank you! And now she is dedicating her life to help others because of what you and Peter did for her. She also loves the hospital and the people she met during the three years she spent there with you."

"Jack, I only did my job and did it the best possible way I knew. Snow wanted to fight to come back. She's a lot like her mother. And there is something I would like to talk to you about also."

"Go right ahead, Ray, you have my full attention."

"During these last six years, I've been corresponding with Patty, as you are aware of. There is a standard of ethics we therapist and doctors observe that we cannot have dual relationships with our patients. And I was careful not to take the role of therapist with Patty, but I was Snow's doctor and became privileged to personal and family history. That is why I have distanced myself for these six years. Also, I knew Patty and Snow needed to heal. I was determined not to jeopardize either one of them by letting my presence get in the way. I had to wait until I felt seeing me would not act as a trigger for regression. But, Jack, from the first second I saw Patty at your home, I loved her. I felt a need to protect her and to share my life with her. During my work with Snow, Patty told me she had feelings for me also, and our feelings cannot be denied."

Jack smiled and said, "Ray, we know! Patty goes on and on about you. She keeps us updated, she can't help it. We know you two are in love."

"And what do you think about that, Jack?" Ray asked.

"I'm on board. I think you are just what the doctor ordered, and actually, he did."

"Can you clarify that for me?" asked Ray.

"Yes," Jack replied. "During one of our many conversations, Peter said that he thought you were the best therapy for Patty. And that he knew your strong sense of ethics would not allow you to act on it."

"Well, Jack, I'm acting on it now, hoping for your blessings?"

"Yes, of course! I couldn't be happier to welcome you to the family as my son-in-law."

"Thank you. We will be making our announcement tomorrow night then."

"Fine with me, Ray, I mean, son!"

Chapter Twenty

Community

The community center was buzzing the next day. The news reporters were there, and it seemed like all of Miami had turned out for the grand opening. The net was exploding and buzzing with the news of the community center. Once inside, everyone had gathered in the community room. Snow took the stage as the official spokeswoman.

"I want to thank you all for being here today to open up this community center. We know that this community and other American communities need intervention for people with mental health problems. At least one out of every four people will experience mental health problems. Most families have at least one member that has or now need services.

This center will address people suffering from grief, eating disorders, victims of abuse, and the chronic mentally ill. Some of these people with chronic mental illness live out their lives on these streets.

As some of you already know that the hotel SANE already turns their café into a warm, welcoming place for the needy to eat breakfast daily. It has become known as the 'Free Standing Breakfast.' Their chef also prepares the food for meals on wheels.

We plan on running a quality, superior soup kitchen. We also will have a pantry that, not only offers food, but we will stock tissues, soaps, and hygiene articles. We also have showers and laundry facilities for those that need them. We have a free store where clothes and other items can be bought with only a thank you.

We hope that this center will not only successfully treat clients with mental illness but assist with the stressors that people endure when they live on the fringe of society. Let us work together to wipe out the stigma that still exist for people wanting to find help. We also will address and help addicts through our 12-step program and therapy.

We also hope to serve the immigrants with their difficult task of assimilating into the American culture. We plan to celebrate and to acknowledge all of the rich, exciting languages, foods, music, dance, traditions, and customs of over 100 different types of households in our community we all call home.

Our center also has a block grant and a public grant from the Martha DuTro foundation, which will enable us to help victims that have been injured or sexually exploited by illegal aliens or victims unable or afraid to get help due to their immigration status.

I want to now thank all the psychiatrist, therapist, social workers, and the mental health staff that works in the field for giving of their time and energy. I thank you all for making this community center a reality and for working to make this community and the world a better place for all.

Now, I would like to thank the people who made this all possible."

Snow read off of a lengthy list. She then invited everyone to take the tour of the Community Center. She was loudly applauded. Snow was very gracious as she answered questions and smiled for the photos.

Snow eventually found her way to Patty, she was standing with Ray. Patty's face was beaming with pride. Duane came up behind Snow and put his arm around her. So, shall we tour. The group of four followed behind as the tour began. The facility was amazing, so well planned out. Once they reached the lobby and the intake room, Ray noticed the painting on the wall. It was a beautiful painting. It was the painting done by the alters. The painting was getting a lot of attention and positive remarks. He heard one person say, "Look at all the signatures, odd?"

Ray thought to himself, yes, you could call the artists odd, but their finished product looks very stunning and is actual a very beautiful painting.

Once back at the hotel, the small group applauded Snow even louder than the people at the ceremony had. Uncle Don and Aunt Louise were seated at the large round table. Attorney Tim and Bob were discussing what they had seen at the community center. Charly was talking to Anna about what a great piece of real estate the community center was setting on. Jack and Joe were talking about some candidates they would like to interview for the hotel.

"Patty," said Ray. "I have decided to take the offer of the director of the community center."

Patty looked up at Ray and replied, "I am so happy. Go on now, it's time!"

Ray took his spoon and tapped his glass, which brought everyone's attention to him. Ray cleared his throat, "Please may I have everyone's attention. As if we haven't had enough excitement today, we are pleased to announce that we are engaged."

Applause and congratulations arose from everyone setting at the table. Patty waited until the clamor subsided.

"Of course, you all are invited to the wedding. We plan to be married on February 14th, you will get your RSVP in the mail very soon. My plan is to be married before my daughter Snow and Duane tie the knot. Now, I must excuse myself, so I can get dressed."

Patty left, and the group at the table waited eagerly for Patty's performance.

Ray thought he knew how beautiful Patty was, but he was not prepared to see her dressed up in pink and turquoise satin. As she took the stage, Ray thought to himself, she is really breath taking! Then she opened up and sang out *I Will Always Love You*. Ray almost lost his balance because he was moved to his very soul by Patty's song. He said aloud she is a real American Star as she ended her song as he clapped, feeling the thunder from the applause that filled the room. Patty smiled and curtsied graciously, trying to calm her fans by moving her hands up and down. Patty finally got the crowd to calm, and she thanked everyone for being there. She told them to enjoy the rest of their night, then welcomed her follow up act, a local DJ, Holy Base.

There was one person in the room who did not clap or celebrate Patty's stellar performance. He sat in the shadows at the table closest to the exit. He was a handsome, middle-aged eastern man who could not take his eyes away from Patty. Once he could break his gaze from her, he quietly slipped away without detection, he thought. But there was someone else, someone who had lived in the shadows himself. Someone that could see into the darkest shadows and shapes, and he recognized Ali, Snow's father.

Jack was enjoying his drink and flirting with his wife when he was interrupted by a call coming in marked urgent. Jack excused himself and took the call. The person on the other end of the line informed him that Ali had been spotted in a photo on the internet. He was in Miami, he was spotted at the Community Center's Opening. Jack's thoughts flashed in his own head. He heard himself saying aloud, "Men like you, Ali, do not value life nor respect women or children. You exist for your own desires to gratify yourselves. You have a depravity, a need for all others to submit to you." Jack thought, I know you, Ali, and I will keep my pockets full of quarters, and my allies with have quarters, too.

Chapter Twenty-One

Unity

It was a nice sunny morning in Miami. There was a pleasant breeze that Patty was enjoying as she walked from her hotel to the community center. She loved the business of Miami and its culture. She had made a lunch for Ray and had planned on eating it with him in his office. As she entered the front doors to the lobby, she saw Snow standing at the reception desk.

"Hello, how's your day been going so far?" Patty asked.

"Well, Mom, it had been pretty uneventful up into like 15 minutes ago," she answered.

"Really, what happened?"

"Come with me," Snow said, tilting her head toward her office.

Patty and Snow walked together into Snow's office. "Mom, normally I would not say anything to you. But a woman and a man came in today while I was out in the community. Anyway, they asked for me personally, Snow DuTro. They told Nancy that they had just arrived from Iran." Patty had been fumbling with the bag she had Ray's and her lunch in until she heard Iran.

She suddenly became more serious and hesitantly told her, "Snow, go on!"

"Well, Mom, the woman would not give her name. But she did say she had seen me in a photo that was taken the day the community center opened."

"Well, that would make sense with the immigrant program here," Patty replied.

Snow was now the stoic one, "Mom, she also asked about you!"

"Well, I'm listed on the marquise and was mentioned as a donor."

"Mom, she asked about Martha DuTro."

Patty was visibly shaken. "What else?" she asked.

"Nancy said the woman and the man seemed nervous and anxious, which Nancy said she thought it was strange because they refused to give any information or even fill out an intake packet. They just left, it seemed, in quite a hurry."

"Snow, we can't tell anyone else about this. With my wedding approaching so soon, I cannot allow anything or anyone to disrupt it. We will take precaution though. Let's make a pact until this thing with these mystery people is solved. We must always be in the company of each other, or someone else from our circle."

"Okay, Mom, I agree, but I also think we need to arm ourselves."

"Yes, Snow, I think you are right. Oh my, I forgot! I had walked from the hotel because it was such a lovely day. I had planned on having lunch with Ray. Not sure about that now, he's pretty good at detecting emotional distress. Even though I'm an expert at masking mine," Patty said as her words drifted off.

"Mom, why don't I just give you a ride home. I need to get my protection out of the safe anyway."

"Sounds like a great idea, let's go!"

* * * *

Once the pair was back at the hotel, Patty asked Snow, "Would you like to have lunch, I had made a nice lunch for Ray?"

"Let's have our lunch in my suite, Mom. I haven't had any real time to spend with you since you announced your engagement. I've been busy at the center, and I've noticed you've been occupied with Ray."

Patty smiled, "Oh yes, I know. We have been planning what rooms we want and what type of décor will be fitting for us as a couple. You know I've been decorating from a female perspective since I bought this hotel. Now I want to include Ray's taste and choice in what will be his home and his private living areas also."

"Oh, that makes perfect sense! Of course, Mom, that's why we haven't seen you for lunch or dinner or cocktail hours. You have been very busy thinking how to decorate your suite."

They both just started laughing. "Great, let's have lunch, Mom. We need to really have a good talk and to catch up."

Patty looked around Snow's rooms. Snow was very tidy, nothing out of place. Snow's rooms were filled with lavender, wicker, seashells, and light swags, which hung brightly around the beautiful floor to ceiling windows. The windows dramatically allowed light into every space in her living room. Snow pushed the wall pad, and the automatic shades closed, and simultaneously, the lights brightened.

"Snow, this is a really a nice look. Do you know if most men like the color lavender?"

"Mom, you are going to have to talk with Ray to discover what colors he likes and what colors he wants to live with. By the way, I thought you two were spending all your time on decorating?"

Patty smiled briefly, "Come on, let's eat and talk."

"So, Mom, what do you think? Who could be the mysterious couple at the center?"

"Snow, I do not know, but it sends chills up my entire body when I think about it."

"Mom, maybe we should tell someone?"

"Well, what are we going to say to them, that two people came to the center asking about us, and they claimed to be from Iran?

Let's just wait until we can try to figure out who these people might be." Just then, the doorbell played *How I Wish You were Here*, and they both jumped.

Snow cautiously went to the door. She felt relief when she saw Anna standing there. "Come on in, Grandma, we were just having a little lunch."

Anna sat down and said, "This is very nice, I am able to see both my beautiful girls together. I saw your car, so I thought I would stop by, and I could pry a little about the wedding. I'm not sure if you were going to be your mother's maid of honor, and if so, where are you shopping at? Sorry, did I interrupt something?" Anna asked as her voice became a whisper.

"No, of course not, Mom. We were just talking about the wedding also."

"Oh, so why are you home so early, Snow?"

"Well, Mom, Snow's car is not running smooth, so she came home early with me."

"Yes, Grandma, I planned on asking Duane for a ride until I can have my car looked at."

"Sounds like an excuse to me!"

"What do you mean, Grandma? I'm not making an excuse, why would you say that?"

"Oh, just thought you might be wanting to spend more time with your handsome fiancée."

"Really, Grandma, you know me too well!" Snow said with a chuckle. Patty just smiled.

"The 14th is coming very soon. What is going to be the color scheme?" Anna went on, "Patty, you are giving up your dream wedding, but tell me you will at least wear white."

"Mom, a dream wedding of a girl of 13 is more like a fantasy. What happened to me changed me. And my aspiration is to be married before my daughter, so she can have the lavish wedding she deserves."

Snow broke in, "Mom, I hate this. You should have the wedding you have always dreamed of."

"Stop it, both of you. The reality is that I have outgrown that daydream for me, but I need this for you, Snow. For your first 16 years of your life, I was not able to be a good mother or even protect you."

"Mom, you did more than I could had ever expected you to do. I was so far away from seeing who you were. You were able to stand for me, you almost died for me, beaten, abused, exploited. No, Mom, you did protect me. I'm strong because of you!"

"Snow, that means so much to me!"

Anna had tears running down her cheeks, then Patty and Snow began to cry and hug.

"I will be married on the 14th here, in this hotel, with my family and dearest friends. I will wear white for you, Mom, and I will be married before you, my dearest daughter, Snow. And I think my colors with be white and ivory. Just as I have said, beautiful new fallen snow to bring about new life."

"Patty, now that we have bought up the topic of mothers protecting daughters. I want your forgiveness because I was not able to protect you!"

"Mom, what are you saying? You sheltered and protected me. He kidnapped me, he is to blame alone, and if I would have told you that an older man was meeting me at the bus, you would have been able to stop it."

Patty and Snow looked at each other. They had the same thought, are we making a mistake by omission?

* * * * *

During the two weeks up to the 14th of February were busy days. Patty and Ray were involved with love making, wedding plans, and completing the white, tan, gold, and ivory color scheme for their penthouse. Snow and Duane were busy at the center, and Snow's car sat in her parking area untouched as she carpooled back and forth from work with Duane. Anna and Jack were busy with the final details of their daughter's wedding.

So, as planned, on the 14th of February, Ray and Patty were wed.

Patty's wedding was beautiful and private. It was attended by her and Ray's family members and closest friends. Anna and Jack were delighted to have seen their daughter married to a good man. Snow was so excited that her mother had found true love, and that she, by the Grace of God, had a father. Patty asked Ray if he thought they could delay their honeymoon to Aruba until the center was opened for at least a few weeks. Ray heartily agreed due to the fact that he was unable to believe that there was a spot-on earth more beautiful than the Hotel SANE. He also shared that it would give him a little time to get settled into his new job there.

During the week that followed, Patty and Snow had almost forgot about the mystery woman. But on a Tuesday, while Snow was walking across the lobby area in the intake room, she suddenly stopped. She couldn't believe her eyes, she saw Joy at the intake window. Snow walked up to the desk and said, "Nancy, I can take it from here."

She motioned for Joy to follow her to a couch, where they both sat down together. Snow looked above her and saw the painting of the Alters.

"What are you doing here, Joy? How dare you come here. You have to leave before my mother sees you. She has suffered too much, and she has a new and unbelievable happy life."

"Snow, I also have suffered."

"Go on, Joy, I'm listening."

"I have been abused and mistreated, both me and my son Omar. We had to flee Iran. I was so hated there. I was mistaken to believe that being Badeel's wife would make me happy."

"Joy, I never understood how you could be so controlled by him. He was so mean."

"Yes, he is so cruel, the whole country is cruel and hateful. Badeel turned against us. It was hard to get back here to the states. If it was not for my son, I would not have been able to ever leave. A woman is only property of her husband. It has been horrible. I also come with a warning."

"What kind of warning?" Snow asked.

"You and Martha are unaware of Ali and Badeel's plans. Ali knows all about you and Martha. He goes back and forth from here to Iran. Before Omar had a falling out with his father, Badeel had told him that both you and Martha were here in Miami. Omar's wife was not able to escape Iran with us."

"Omar is married?"

"Yes, and she is still at Badeel's house. Omar talks with her every night. Omar is fearful that Badeel might harm her. She's the one that told us that Martha was getting married. She told Omar she had overheard Ali and Badeel talking about trying to stop the wedding. She said they decided to wait until after the wedding, thinking it was too dangerous to attempt the coup in Miami. We knew from my daughter-in-law that you and Martha were safe until after the wedding. We thought it was best to wait. Badeel doesn't know we are here. We are in hiding and need your help!"

Snow started to feel dizzy. She asked Joy to wait for a moment as she went to her office. As she looked up while heading to her office, she thought she saw the pizza spin and move across the painting.

Snow went to her office and cried. She then picked up the phone and called her mother, "Mom, I know who the mystery woman is. Please sit down and let me know when you are sitting." After waiting a few seconds, she went on to say, "Mom, it is Joy." Another pause, then she continued, "Mom, she said she had to flee Iran. Yes, Joy. She is here at the center right now. She said that Omar is here, too. No, he is not at the center with her right now. No, I do not know where they are staying. Yes, she seems scared. I do believe her. And Mom, she said that

Ali and Badeel have been watching us. She said they know everything about us. Yes, and she said they knew about the wedding. She said she wants our help and that she knew she had to warn you. Alright then, I am going to bring Joy back to my office and wait until you and Grandpa can get here. Okay, see you in a few minutes, love you, bye."

❖ ❖ ❖ ❖ ❖

Patty was able to quickly fill Jack in on Joy and the details she had found out from Snow. They arrived at the center within minutes. Jack told Nancy that they were there to see Snow. She told them to go ahead as she buzzed them into Snow's office.

Jack put his hand on the door knob before Patty could open it. He looked at his daughter and said, "Patty, breathe and clear your head before going in. A ghost from your past is waiting in that room."

"I know, Dad, and Snow is in there alone with her right now." Patty pushed open the door and there sat an aged Joy.

Snow motioned them both in. "I already called Ray. He is coming as soon as his current session ends."

Patty walked over to Joy, and the two old friends hugged. "Can I have a few minutes alone with Joy?" Snow and Jack both agreed.

"We'll be in the cafeteria, just text me if you need us, Mom," said Snow as they left the room.

Patty turned to Joy. "Snow told me what's been happening with you and Omar, but I need to hear the whole story from you."

"Martha."

Patty interrupted, "There is no Martha here. My name is Patty now. I am the adopted daughter of Jack and Anna DuTro. Martha is dead."

"Oh, I see," said Joy. Breathing in heavily, Joy started again. "Patty, the life I thought I was going to have in Iran was a hoax. I thought I wanted to be a wife that submitted to her husband. I should have realized that a woman can only truly submit to a man if he is honorable. My father was an honorable man, and he loved my mother. That is what I thought I had in my marriage. But the world changed. I don't think that the world can sustain marriages like the one my parents had. My mom submitted to my father, but my father loved her, so he always put her needs and her well-being before his own. My mom used to say, 'Your father is the head of this house, and I'm the neck.' Funny, I found out while in Iran that my husband might want to separate my head from my neck. Patty, I've been through hell, both me and my poor son Omar."

Patty gave Joy a hug. "Go ahead, I'm listening."

"I had been in denial believing that Badeel was a man trapped in his radical beliefs, but it's his radical politics that enslaves. He does not deem worth in other people's lives. He only desires submission. I thought that he loved me as a woman and desired me. He only wanted me as a replacement for his mother. He wanted a woman to meet all of his domestic needs, to run his house, and to blindly obey and submit. I really loved him and wanted to be a good wife and mother. He has never really cared about me, I know that now."

"I'm sorry," said Patty.

"As an American Muslin, I was hated in Iran. I was often spit on, kicked, and slapped when I went to the market. One day, some of the women there were ganging up on me. They began beating me with their fist and pulling my hair. When my daughter in-law saw what was happening, she intervened. She herself was kicked and threatened by those hateful women. We were able to get away. I remember I was so happy to be back at my home. I felt safe. I had a blackeye and a cut lip. I told Badeel what had happened and asked if I could send one of our servants to the market instead of me going there any longer." Joy's sobs became louder.

Patty comforted her, "It's okay, you are here with a friend, and you are safe. Please, go on when you can."

"He told me no, that I needed to go myself and beg the other women to forgive me for being born in America. He told me I needed to declare my alliance to Iran and curse America. I told him I was still an American, and I had family still in the states. He beat me himself then. He would not stop until I cursed America and my parents for being American citizens."

"Joy, that is sad, but you knew what a brutal man he was before you moved to Iran."

"I know, it's like I said, I thought he was like that because of his beliefs. I didn't want to judge him for his religious ideas. I did not understand that his politics and values judged me and that there was no place for disagreement."

"Omar is here, is his wife here also?" asked Patty.

"No, Irma is not here. Patty, I came to love her as my own daughter. After I was so badly beaten at the market, she would not let me go back. She went for me. Omar loves her so much. That is why Badeel turned against him. He wanted Omar to marry again because Irma couldn't get pregnant. Omar refused because he loves Irma. So, Badeel and Omar began to argue more and more."

"I'm sorry."

"They never agree on politics or religion. Omar says his wants are simple, that he believes in being happy and seeking a peaceful life. Well, you know what Badeel wants, submission of others, unrestrained power, and an unbridled pursuit for his selfish desires. Patty, we need your help. When we escaped, Irma didn't make it out."

"Go on, but I don't know how I can help?"

"Well, we were able to get a taxi to the airport. We had our passports, and Irma had her passport and her visa, but the officials would not let her board. We were forced to leave because we were Americans. This all happened about two weeks ago."

"I see," Patty said as she continued to listen intently.

"Badeel is still out of the country, we think he is in Egypt. We need help to get her out before he comes home and discovers we have left. There is no telling what Badeel might do to her. They will use her as a pawn to get us back. Once we go back, Badeel will take his revenge." Joy broke down sobbing.

"And where is Ali?" Patty asked.

Joy continued, "He comes over nightly. Irma has been lying. She told him that we are sick with some horrible virus, so he hasn't asked to see us. But this can't go on much longer. Even though Omar and Irma are married, there is no help. She tried to get help from the Swiss Embassy, but they were not able to help her. They said they have been talking to the Americans trying to get her on a flight though."

"Incredible, that poor girl. I know firsthand what it's like to be under their power."

"We can't let anyone know that we are here," Joy told her.

"Okay, I believe you, Joy. How was Ali able to discover where Snow and I were at?"

"Patty, while Ali was here, he did some intensive networking. He has many connections, there is an entire underground system that flourishes without detection. He is plugged into this vast network. They have people in high ranking positions throughout the entire country. What a different world we would be living in today if Hitler had the foreknowledge to indoctrinate the youth of the free world in their colleges and in the universities. The fabric has already been woven, the Islamic influence, their beliefs, their propaganda, and their opposition to American freedoms are now and forever part of the American landscape."

"Yes, I knew he had many connections," said Patty.

"Ali is just one actor in these events. He even has someone on staff in your hotel that is an informant. They keep him updated on all of your moves and activities. He knew about your wedding, he knew that you had planned a trip for your honeymoon." The women jumped when they heard a knock at the door. Patty heard Ray's voice as he said, "Coming in!"

Ray opened the door and walked in with Snow and Jack following behind.

"Dad and Ray, I would like to introduce you to Joy, my one-time guard, and now, I hope my lifetime friend."

Patty explained how after Snow's escape and her miscarriage that Joy attended to her and, "I believe Joy saved my life, not only with the medical attention she gave me then, but Joy did give me the valiums, which was the lone means for my escape."

Jack looked sternly at Joy and asked, "Joy, you can understand why we are suspicious of you?"

"Yes, I do understand. You don't know me or my son, but I can assure you I stand unified with you. I need your help just as you need ours."

"Please clarify why we would need your help?"

"When we arrived, we came here the first day to warn Patty and Snow and ask for help."

Interjecting, Ray said, "Excuse me, you were here over a week ago."

"Yes, before the wedding," she told him.

"Patty, did you know about this?"

Snow jumped in, "Yes, Ray, Mom and I both knew that a woman and her son came to the center asking about us. We decided to wait till after the wedding before talking to anyone."

"That was pretty darn foolish, Patty," Ray interrupted. "I told you that your father and I needed to know immediately if there was even a sign or hint that this villain Ali might be lurking about."

Patty looked to her father and said, "Dad, I'm sorry, really. I didn't think it was anything alarming."

Ray gave Patty an exasperating look, "Okay, Joy, where is your son now?"

"He is at our hotel. We are staying just a few blocks away."

"This is what we need to do," said Jack, "you call him and ask him to come here. I think for the time being it's best if you both stay with us at hotel SANE."

"I'm only hesitant because there is a spy there who is in constant contact with Ali," explained Joy.

"We will be very secretive," Jack said assuring. "We will bring you in our private entrance. Trust me, only people from our closest circle will know anything about you or your son. We will protect you. Both you and your son will be safe with us until we can figure out our next step."

"Joy, when did you first hear anything about Ali knowing where Patty was at," asked Ray.

"It was about a few weeks before the wedding. Irma said she had overheard them speaking in Persian, they often forget that she is a native. Anyway, that is when she overheard Ali talking to Badeel about wanting to stop the wedding. Badeel convinced him not to interfere. Then Irma told Omar a couple of days ago that she heard Ali on the phone telling Badeel that Martha had cancelled her honeymoon plans. They had planned to do something during the honeymoon while they were outside of the U.S."

"Go on now and call your son," encouraged Snow. Joy called Omar, he met her at the center, and within 30 minutes, they were both safely hidden away at SANE the very private guest of the DuTro's.

Snow felt exhausted by the time she reached her rooms. She threw herself down on her sofa and cried. After she had a good cry, she reached for the phone to call Duane. "Duane, I've had an emotional day. Can you please come over and bring your tooth brush and any work you will need with you tomorrow?"

Snow was still sitting on her sofa in the same position when her doorbell rang out *How I Wish You were Here*. On hearing her door bell's chime, Snow jumped up and ran to the door. She flung the door open and fell into Duane's arms.

"What's the matter, baby? You left early, are you sick?" he asked.

"Just come on in and pull up a chair. Today, a ghost from the past has caught up with us." Duane and Snow walked toward the sofa with their arms wrapped around each other.

"Snow, what has happened?"

"Let me get you a beer before I begin." Snow got up and went to the refrigerator and grabbed them both a beer. She opened Duane's beer and handed it to him while taking a sip herself. She then looked down at Duane.

"Duane, that's the same look you had the first day I met you. Remember we were at the lecture on the use of CB. I saw you sitting in the first row, and I decided that I wanted to sit in the seat next to you. I remember approaching the seat when there was a flurry. Then I sat down next to you, and you had the same look you have in your eyes right now. What is that look?"

"Oh, definitely surprise!" he said.

"Oh, you were surprised when I sat next to you during the lecture. Then, too?"

"No, it was when you told the girl that was sitting there to get up, that she had taken your seat. Then you sat down, and your forwardness surprised me."

"What are you talking about?" Snow said with a nervous laugh. "Your memory is so not true."

"Snow, I remember the first day I saw you and every detail exactly."

"Duane, you are so wrong! No one had taken that seat next to you. We were all walking toward the seats we wanted."

"Oh, no, no, no!" Duane was interrupted by a phone call coming in on Snow's phone.

Snow held up her finger and said, "This is Grandpa, I have to take it."

"Grandpa, Duane is here with me right now. Yes, I was just getting ready to fill him in. Okay, bye for now."

Duane asked, "What's going on?"

"That was Grandpa, I got off track. Today, my father's brother's wife, my aunt, came into the community center needing help." Snow then caught Duane up on everything that was said during the meeting with Joy. She then went on to inform him that Joy and Omar were secret guests at the hotel.

"Wow, all of this craziness today must had been a real shock for you, Snow. How are you?"

"Shook up, and I had a few minutes of memory loss."

"This must be really tough for you and your family. What a lot of stress for everyone. Don't freak out about spacing out for a few minutes."

"Duane, I'm really stressed. I am going to tell you something, but you can't tell anyone, I do not want anyone, especially my mom, to over react."

"Tell me, come on, you know I'm not reactive. So, tell me, what is it?"

"When I was first talking with Joy, I had a small hallucination."

"Tell me what it was?" he asked.

"I was sitting on the couch talking with Joy, and when I got up to go to my office, I looked up at the picture, you know the one that the Alters painted? Well, I saw the pizza spin and move."

"Snow, that's just because you have been working long hours and this woman showing up after all of this time was a shock to your system. Listen, your mom just got married. We just opened the center. You have even been doing home visits. Babe, you just need some time off. I think you should consider at least a few days off. Let's deal with this stress positively."

"I can't just leave my clients right now, and you know we have just got the programs up and running."

"Snow, you just had a glitch. We all have that type of interference sometimes. If you're not going to take a few days off, promise me you will slow down some."

"Duane, this hallucination really shook me. You know all about my past. Duane, I was so ill, and I lost my grasp on reality! Then to be declared sane and in good health. You know what I had to go through to get my licenses."

"Babe, I know it was hard."

She continued, "I had to sit in front of the board proving my mental health status. I had to prove that my therapy had been effective. I needed Dr. Rose to give me a recommendation, and I had to have that open-ended discussion convincing the board that all of my issues were resolved. And now I see a pizza moving in a picture!"

"Snow, take some time off!"

"With everything going on at the center, I can't take off. But what if I'm not okay? What if I slip back?"

"Come over here, you just need a big bear hug." Snow moved closer to Duane. "Snow, you're fine," Duane said as he ran his fingers down her face with a loving touch. "This was just a stressful day and very upsetting. Seeing Joy just triggered you. You're okay. You just got upset, as you said, a ghost showed up today! So, what does Jack want?"

"He's gathering the people loyal to Patty. He feels that we need to act or at least be prepared for whatever Ali is planning. He has a strategy meeting plan for tomorrow night at 6 pm."

"Where?" he asked.

"In the Habana room. He said dinner is on him. "

"Tell him I'll be there," Duane said, smiling.

"I plan on being there, too."

"Snow, I don't think your grandpa wants you to attend. He's pretty protective of you."

"Well, I'm going." Snow snuggled up to Duane and gave him a deep kiss.

Duane then picked Snow up and headed for the bedroom. "Let's talk tomorrow; for now, I think you need some loving."

Patty was doing some back peddling, too. "Ray, I did not think there was anything to be concerned about. I just wanted our wedding to be free from any shadows from the past."

"Patty, I understand that, but I need to know the facts. Logically, we need information in order to act wisely in any given situation. It's when information is left out and things that are hidden become dangerous. Logically, you would have shared the information with the people that love you and want to protect you. But you acted out of emotions."

"Ray, I'm sorry, please don't analyze me. I promise to inform you on any and all information regarding this horrible situation with Ali and Badeel that I learn from this moment on."

"Good, enough said. Your dad is calling a meeting. He wants to bring everyone together to examine this situation and to plan our actions. Are you going to attend?"

"Yes, I think I need to be there. I am a little worried about Snow. I hope she stays back. She looked so tired."

"She is a hard worker and so dedicated to her clients. Maybe she will listen if her mother tells her to get some rest."

"I try not to tell anyone what to do, but I'll give her a call and ask her to have coffee with me in the morning."

"Patty, I wanted to ask you if you are still planning on entertaining and being the opening act. I know you have already booked some really good groups to fill in for you while we were on our honeymoon."

"Yes, and I have them under contract for the opening acts. I have already booked some very exciting acts. And I was thinking that we should still go on a honeymoon."

"Really, I think that is just what the doctor ordered. And where would you like to go?"

I had wanted that tropical Aruba honeymoon, but with the risk from Ali, I've been thinking that we need to stay closer to home within the states. And talking about home, I thought that maybe we need to go back home. Ray, you could see your aunt and sister. Plus, I would like to see Tina, she has always been like an aunt to me. And we can go to Gate's and eat some real barbeque."

"Now that sounds like a honeymoon to me, count me in. And what are we going to do for the second week?" Duane asked.

"Let's come back here and hide out. Let's make wild, crazy love!"

"Sounds great, when do we leave?"

Patty was out on her veranda when Snow joined her for coffee in the morning. "Mom, I think everyone felt a little hurt because we didn't tell them that a mystery couple from Iran was asking about us."

"Yes, I've heard it all myself from Grandma, Grandpa, and Ray. But I would not have ever thought Joy would have left Iran."

"Mom, are you sure you can trust her? I feel uneasy. She lied to me all those years, and I hardly know Omar. He was a cool kid, and I liked playing with him when Joy brought him over. But I feel so uncomfortable knowing that Ali has a mole here at the hotel if we can believe what she is saying?"

"Snow, after your escape, we became close. Joy saw herself as a prisoner, too. She had no place to go. Her parents would not take her and Omar in. I know she was afraid of Badeel, and yet, she said she loved him."

"Mom, do you think a woman can fear her husband and love him at the same time?"

"I think that Joy compartmentalized her relationship with Badeel. But to answer your first question, yes, I trust her. To your second question, women have been loving men they fear forever. Snow, you look so tired. How about spending some time with me just relaxing? Let's spend the day on the beach."

"That's sounds like a great idea. I am exasperated, but I'm all booked up on my schedule."

"No, you're not. Duane called and said that the schedule had been cleared."

"Really? Good, Mom. I do need a day off, and I would love a beach day with you."

CHAPTER TWENTY-TWO

BONUS WEEKEND

Jack welcomed his guests to the reserved Habana room. Anna made Philly cheese sandwiches and poppers with chips and beer. Ray and Duane were among Jack's family and friends in attendance. Uncle Don, Attorney Tim, Bob, Charley, and Joe all were there. Jack explained what had transpired with Joy and Omar. He then informed them that there was a mole, and they were not sure who it was. He had made a list of the SANE's staff that had knowledge about the wedding prior to the actual date of the wedding.

He read off of his list of employees, "Fred, Chef, Dalir, manager, George, night manager, Sara, my assistant, Carlos, head waiter, Sandy, cocktail waitress, and Steve, waiter."

"Jack," questioned Uncle Don, "so what is the plan? Do you plan on meeting with these people?"

"Yes, I plan on holding private meetings with each one of these individuals."

Anna interjected, "My mom always told me you can catch a bee with honey."

"Okay, Anna, what are you thinking?" Jack asked.

"I'm thinking that most of our staff is like our family, and they are good, hardworking people. I do not want to offend anyone."

"Yes, I know that is true, Anna, but we have to know who the spy is and how Ali got his information."

Tim broke in, "We can have them come to my office for a deposition."

"We need to be cautious. We have to maintain Patty's identity, so what information we give them needs to be very limited."

Just then, Patty and Snow walked in. "Sorry we are late. Time got away from us while we were on the beach."

"Didn't think you two were coming!" Jack said. "I was sure we all thought it might be a little hard for both of you."

"Dad, of course we had planned on being here. And yes, I will address the white elephant. This is very emotional and stressful for both of us. We have talked about it, and we are okay and that is because we have all of you. We have the support and love of everyone in this room. So, we are just going to take our seats," Patty said as she and Snow sat down.

"Okay, what I was saying about honey is that I think we should have a weekend to celebrate our loyal, hardworking hotel employees. I was thinking we can tell them that we want to reward them with a stay here. They can enjoy all the perks and amenities of the hotel, they and their family members. This will give us a great opportunity to talk with them individually, observe them, reward them with a bonus, and not to be punitive or accusative to the innocent."

"Sounds like a great idea, does anyone else have any more input?" asked Jack.

Patty said, "I love this idea. I say yeah."

"Okay then, how many yeahs do we have? All yeahs!" Everyone in the room agreed it was a great idea and stood united. The group then reviewed the information from the investigator, which did not give the group any real valuable information considering what they already knew, that Ali and Badeel were still on the terrorist list.

Ray then took the floor. "I just want to update everyone about our honeymoon plans. We are not going out of the states. Our plan is to spend a week travelling and sightseeing until we end up in Missouri, with our last night staying in Kansas City. Then to spend the next week of our honeymoon back here. We will wait to make our final plans for Missouri after the staff's bonus week, then we will let you know the details. The issue I'm having with all of this is that we plan on being very involved and not busy with anything other than what people usually do on their honeymoons."

"So, you plan on eating a lot of wedding soup!" Joe said with a chuckle. "Isn't that what people usually do on their honeymoon?"

Then everyone laughed. "Okay, yes, we will be very busy on our honeymoon eating wedding soup." Everyone laughed again. Ray held out his hands, moving them up and down, trying to quiet the room. Once the laughter died down, Ray went on, "However, Patty will call Anna every night, so all will know that all is good."

Tim and Joe busted out laughing again. Jack shook his head, "Come on, let's eat up. Anna has made us a feast." That night, they all feasted and enjoyed just being with people they loved and trusted.

* * * * *

The next day, early in the morning, Badeel was woken up by the ringing of his private phone. The voice was that of his contact at hotel SANE.

"Hello, yes, you need to get ready to make your move. Martha and her husband will be in Missouri within weeks."

"That's good news!" Badeel replied. "I have connections and inroads there."

"Yes, I know, remember, so do I."

"Will Snow be with them?"

"No, not sure at this time if the daughter will also travel to Missouri. I will keep you informed and updated."

Badeel smiled as he hung up the phone, feeling self-assured that his plan was coming together.

• • • • •

Jack was busy in his office, also feeling confident. He made the arrangements to meet with the selected staff. Once all the staff was in the Habana room, he rolled out his plan.

"Hello, I would like to thank you all for attending this special meeting. Your work and customer service are greatly appreciated and valued by hotel SANE and me. Hotel SANE has selected the best of our staff, and if you are in this room, you are one. We would like to honor you with a bonus weekend. You will receive your regular hourly pay while you and your immediate family members have a free weekend stay. All of your meals will be on SANE. You can enjoy all of the amenities, and we will give you $200 of hotel's SANE cash to use anywhere on the grounds. This is our way to thank you for your loyalty and service."

Jack waited as the room clapped and shouted for joy.

"I would like to meet with each of you individually to answer any questions you may have and to book your free stay here. You have been scheduled, and you have a card with the time on it. So, please stop by my office on the time allotted on your card. Thank you all again." The staff heartily applauded.

• • • • •

The first staff member to meet with Jack was Steve. "So, Steve, tell me a little about yourself."

"Mr. DuTro, I have been a server here for three years, and I love my job. I feel honored to work here, and SANE treats me very well."

"That's good to hear, Steve. Are you married?"

"No, not married"

"I hear that you were born in Miami?"

"Yes, I am a native of Miami."

"Steve, who do you plan on bringing with you?"

"Mr. DuTro, my mother, and I also have a good friend I would like to invite."

"That's fine, we will give you a suite with three bedrooms. Do you have any other questions for me, Steve?"

"No, Mr. DuTro, I just want to thank you." They shook hands, and Steve returned to work.

❋ ❋ ❋ ❋

He met next with Carlos. "How long have you been with us?" Jack asked.

"Since you opened, Mr. DuTro."

"Good man, so tell me what types of accommodations will you need?"

"I plan on bringing my wife, our four kids, and our dog "

"That's sounds like you will have a real family vacation."

"I am looking forward to this weekend."

"So, Carlos, are you originally from Miami?"

"No, I am from Cuba. I have been here for about ten years. We love America and Miami. My family will be so happy. My children asked me about the palace all the time. They call the hotel the palace."

"We want to make sure they have a really good time and can take away some happy memories from their weekend here. I have you booked in one of the pet friendly suites. Is there anything else you would like to ask me, Carlos?"

"No, sir, and thank you."

❋ ❋ ❋ ❋

"Fred, I'm so happy to meet with you. Your performance here as head chef is stellar. We also appreciate the work you do with the free-standing breakfast and Meal on Wheels. We hope you and your family will enjoy this weekend."

"Jack, this is great because we were just talking. It was about time we both needed a getaway. My girlfriend, Cheyenne, has just finished her MBA, and she worked so hard, she deserves a break. It will only be the two of us. We need to spend time alone."

"Sounds like you need the honeymoon package."

"Jack, that would be an awesome gift for the both of us! She is going to be so excited! I can't thank you and hotel SANE enough."

* * * * *

"Hello, Dalir. I'm glad you were able to arrange your schedule to meet with me after all."

"Mr. DuTro, what you are doing for us is just amazing. I have some anxiety though. I'm a little hesitant because I have a partner, her name is Alex."

"Dalir you know our policy here, we welcome everyone. We have never denied any service to any group of people. That goes for people in same sex relationships. I can't wait to meet her during the bonus weekend, and let Alex know that I'm looking forward to meeting her."

* * * * *

"George, so what do you think about the bonus weekend?" asked Jack.

"I'm pretty pumped up about spending a weekend here as a guest."

"Will Nettie be coming? I have never been able to have a real conversation with her when she comes to pick you up from work."

"Of course, Jack. She is going to be so excited when I tell her. My parents will be here from Georgia that weekend. My dad is coming to be the guest speaker at the Vineyard church. Would it be okay if I invite my mother and father?"

"I'll be glad to meet them."

"They are curious about my job and what I do. You won't mind?"

"No, of course not. George, it's a family get away," Jack smiled and gave George a pat on the back.

* * * * *

Sandy was so excited when she met with Jack. She told him that her four children were going to be so happy.

"Mr. DuTro, my children have never been on a real vacation. We only spend vacations with family members. I was planning on inviting my sister and her two children."

"Sounds like you and your family are going to have a great time visiting with each other," Jack told her. "We will put you in a first-floor suite. Then the children will be able to walk directly out onto the beach."

* * * * *

Sara was the last to meet with Jack. "So, Sara, are you excited about the bonus weekend?"

"Yes, Jack. My husband and myself will love being treated as your special guests. I have already booked the Del Prado's as the opening act that weekend, knowing that Patty will still be enjoying her honeymoon."

"Sara, have you had a chance to talk with Patty about that?"

"No, not as yet."

"Make sure you can get with her before she leaves. So, Sara, I suppose it's time to get back to work, how about you? Are you ready to get back to work on this beautiful, lovely day?"

"Is that a trick question, how should I answer my boss?"

"No need to answer, I'll answer for you. I don't feel much like going back to work today either. Matter of fact, put on the out of office message, and let's just call it quits for the day, after you follow up with Patty. Are you in agreement?"

"Sounds good to me! I'll take care of closing."

• • • • •

It was such beautiful weather for the bonus staff weekend. As the guests arrived, they were checked in, then given time to relax until they attended the dinner planned and given in their honor. After the dinner, the entire party went out on the beach to watch the glorious sun set. As the sun set behind the city, the group applauded. The sun seemed to say thanks by leaving beautiful colors of turquoise, lavender, pinks, and golds in the setting skies. Once the sun had set, they all departed from the beach. Each going to their own predetermined destinations and activities. The staff were all excited and they were enjoying their night at hotel SANE.

Jack's group did not go to play but met together. Each person there picked from a hat, drawing out a name of one of Hotel SANE's staff.

"Okay, remember the name on that slip of paper. That name is the person you will get to know and befriend this weekend. Get to work. Be friendly and investigative. We will meet again Monday. Be prepared to make a judgement and have the evidence to back it up."

The Monday after staff bonus week, Jack's group met in the Habana Room. Ray was seated first at the table, so he went first.

"Chef Fred is an activist. He is committed first to his family, then to his community, his employer, and he is very loyal to Hotel SANE. He is not the mole."

"I feel that I need to go next," stated Tim. "Dalir is from Iran." As he said the words, the room went silent. Everyone's eyes were fixed on Tim. "She left Iran due to the persecution. She talked about cruelty and the injustice she saw inflicted on people who were gay and living the alternative lifestyles. Anyway, she came to the states on a student visa and then applied for citizenship. She has family back in Iran."

The room went up in a drone of noise and small talk.

Jack spoke up, "Let us all settle down and continue as planned."

Uncle Don spoke next, "George is from Georgia. He comes from hardworking, religious people. His father and mother are devoted to him. He's a good man, I do not believe he would ever betray anyone or be a spy. He is too honest!"

Duane spoke next, "Your assistant Sara is very constricted in her emotions. She is guarded. She also has knowledge of all the comings and goings here at Hotel SANE. She is suspicious and a suspect."

Joe said, "I'll go next. Sandy is from Puerto Rico. She is hardly making ends meet. Life is difficult for her as she struggles with money. But she has a lot of self-respect. No, she would never do anything to hurt anyone. She's not the mole."

Bob said, "We do not have to worry about Steve, he's a good kid. Very honest young man. He is a very hard worker, not a mole."

Charly went next, "Carlos is from Cuba. He is a hardworking man also with strong morals. No threat, very straight forward. He does not have the characteristics of a traitor."

"Good job. I thank everyone for their hard work and commitment to this weekend. I feel that we need to concentrate on Dalir and Sara," Jack commented. "Okay, let's focus on Dalir first."

Tim spoke up, "Where do we go from here?"

"We need someone to follow up with her, right?" asked Snow.

"Who should follow up with her?" questioned Jack.

Tim looking around at the others, said, "Jack, we think you should. You are her boss. Do I have a yeah?" All yeahs were heard throughout the room.

"I accept. I do not want to hesitate though. I'll meet with her once we conclude this meeting." Jack then thanked everyone for attending.

Back in his office, Jack told Sara to hold his calls and to send word that he needed to meet with Dalir. Within minutes, Dalir entered Jack's office with a bright smile on her face.

"Mr. DuTro, I can't thank you enough for the wonderful time Alex and I had during the bonus weekend."

Jack replied in a monotone voice, "Glad you enjoyed yourself." He went on to say, "You probably are wondering why I have asked you here."

"Well, yes, I'm a little curious, Mr. DuTro."

"Well, it concerns my daughter, Patty. She holds a majority of the shares in Hotel SANE. You would not know this, but she was kidnapped once and that man was from Iran. He is presently on the no-fly list and is identified as a terrorist. He also has a brother, Badeel." Dalir gasped, and the color drained from her face.

"Oh, no, Mr. DuTro! I hope I have not caused Patty any problems, but I feel that I need to tell you something." Clearing her voice, Dalir took a deep breath and began. "About a month ago, I received a call from an anonymous caller. His voice was masked. He told me he knew I was from Iran, and he knew that I had family there. He then asked me if I could get someone's number for him that lived in Iran. I asked him why, and he said that he had a family member in Iran and wanted to contact him. He told me he would give me $2,000 if I could get the number. He also told me I had two weeks and that he would call me back. He said if I was able to give him the number when he called back that he would send me a cashier's check. I told him I would try and that I would contact my brother. The name of the man he was trying to get in contact with was Badeel Hame." Taking another breath, she continued, "My brother was able to find this Badeel, and he gave me his number."

"Did you yourself talk to Badeel?"

"No, Mr. DuTro, only to this man. He did send me the $2,000 cashier check. I'm sorry, I did not think it had anything to do with this hotel or Ms. Patty."

"Dalir, weren't you concerned, or did you question why this man had masked his voice and wanted a person's telephone number from Iran?"

"No, Mr. DuTro. We are not a free people. We live under persecution and death threats. I was not concerned that he was secretive. Sometimes we who left family members there are blackmailed and are made to pay a ransom to keep them safe. We all have to be careful what we say. If we say something negative about Iran publicly, our family members are often threatened or harmed, sometimes killed. I thought he was concerned for one of his family members. If a man from Iran would have called me and asked me for someone's number or address here in America, I know my alarm would have gone off. I would have felt something was wrong, and I would not have given him any information. Has something bad happened?"

"No, just what I told you. They have tried to find out information about Patty."

"Again, I'm so sorry. Will you call homeland security and tell them about me?"

"No, no, Dalir, but you must tell me if this man tries to contact you again."

"Of course, Mr. DuTro, I promise."

Dalir, I also need to ask you to keep this information confidential and not to speak to anyone of this. Patty's life might be in jeopardy."

"Of course, I will not speak of this to anyone. Mr. DuTro, I'm from Iran, I know about being silent to survive. I do feel shaken and a little fearful."

"Don't be worried, they just want to find Patty. You're safe here, and we will watch out for you. Call me if you or Alex feels threatened," Jack said as he patted Dalir's hand.

Jack went home early again, thinking to himself, this whole affair with Ali and Badeel is getting the best of me. This pressure seems like it is building inside my head. Why was this man allowed in our country in the first place? Now he comes and goes as he pleases and spies on our lives after all the harm he has done. That poor woman, Joy, and her son had to go into hiding. What kind of country do we live in? I can't even protect my family, Jack shouted in his own head.

Anna could tell that Jack was feeling pressured when he walked through the door by just one glance at his face. "Jack, you're home early. Come sit over here, talk to me as I massage your back."

"Thanks, Anna, I can really use that right now," Jack said as he sat down next to Anna. "I'm just having a difficult time dealing with this Ali and his brother. I hate to say it, but I keep thinking that Martha, oops, I mean, Patty. I think she should have injected him with the whole syringe. We can't even call our daughter by her given birth name because of a monster."

"Jack, we have been through worse. Just think back to the days when we were hopeless. The days we thought we would never see our baby again. We made it through that because we were able to lean on each other and help each other. And now, we have our daughter and her baby."

"I know, you're right, it just gets overwhelming," Jack said. "Remember we decided back then not to be victims. We decided that we would fight to change what we could while accepting the reality of the situation. Once we started practicing that model, we were able to move beyond our misery back into hope."

"You're right, Anna. I would not have made it without you. Your magic hands and sensibility have cured me once again. Okay then, let's call the girls, I need to fill you all in. Then we will go and talk to Joy."

❖ ❖ ❖ ❖

SNOW AT THE DOME

The whole DuTro clan, including Ray and Duane, went to talk with Joy. Joy invited them in.

When Omar saw Snow, he told her he was delighted to see her again. Thinking back, he remembered her as a little girl, someone from his childhood. He smiled, remembering his green-eyed cousin. "Snow, do you remember how I used to kid you about your nose. I would say your nose looked like a bird's beak. Then you would chase me and hit me with your fist, saying I'm going to peck you."

"Indeed, I do remember that," she answered. "And then I would tell you that a short little boy like you needed to respect girls that were taller and smarter."

"I guess we both liked to tease each other back then. And now my cousin Snow is so grown up," Omar said ,smiling at Snow. "As a little boy, I thought your life was perfect because you had your dad and you lived in a big house."

She replied with, "And I thought your life was perfect because your mom was not sick, and your dad did not live with you."

Patty smiled and said, "You both had hard childhoods, but look at what wonderful people you are today. And you both have found someone you love and want to share your lives with. Snow, you have Duane, and Omar, you have Irma."

"Sorry we came over so late," apologized Jack, "but we discovered that someone contacted Badeel. Someone arranged to get his number through a staff member of the hotel. Omar, have you heard from Irma?"

"Yes, she was able to call last night. We, Mom and I, were going to let you know what happened," said Omar, looking at his mother. "Irma told me that Badeel hit her when he returned home from Egypt. She said he tried to make her tell him where we were, but she refused. She also told me that Badeel said that she had conspired against him, and he was going to bring charges against her. Irma said she barricaded herself in her room until Badeel went out. Irma was able to use the phone to call her mother. She told her mother everything. She told her what Badeel said and did to her. Her mother agreed that she could go back home until she was able to leave Iran for America. Then she made Irma's father go and face Badeel. He told Badeel that he needed his daughter to come home and take care of his wife because she was ill. Badeel argued, but because Irma's father went to him and told him that he needed his daughter to return home to take care of his wife, Badeel had to let her go. So, Irma is safe for now."

Jack smiled, and everyone agreed that they were happy to hear that Irma was safe.

Omar went on to say, "Irma also said that Badeel received a phone call the day he returned home and that she thought it was unusual because he was speaking English. She said she listened and heard him say the name Snow. She also said he went into another room and closed the door, so she could not over hear."

"Interesting," said Jack

"Jack, I hope that will help. I know that Irma needs to leave Iran as soon as possible before things close in on her. When do you think Immigration will let Irma come here? She won't be able to stay at her mother's too much longer."

"Omar, we have our friends working on it. We will get her out. We have filed a petition under religious persecution because she is a Christian." Jack then told Joy and Omar about Dalir and the phone call from an unknown person. He told them that the caller sent $2,000 to her and that she had gave the caller Badeel's number.

Joy said, "This can only be more trouble if Snow's name was mentioned."

Duane felt a lump in his throat as he said, "I agree with you. Snow, I think you need to call off work. Maybe you can go to Missouri with your mom?"

"Really! Duane, do you think Ray and Mom want me there on their honeymoon?"

Patty moved closer to Snow. "Honey, we don't care. We would love to have you go with us to Missouri. This hasn't been a real honeymoon for us since we heard that Ali and Badeel were planning something. We will go on a real honeymoon after all of this is behind us. Plus, I would not worry as much if you're with us."

"I can't agree with your mom more, we would love your company," added Ray.

"Okay, Ray, I guess everyone has convinced me. But if we are both gone, who will take care of our work at the center?"

"Snow, I can handle that. I don't want to take chances, they might have your entire routine down," Duane told her.

"Duane is right," interjected Jack.

"Okay, okay, I feel foolish. A grown woman tagging along with her mother on her honeymoon! But I will agree if we can spend some time in Kansas City to see the Kansas City Chiefs and the Kansas City Royals stadiums."

"You got it," said Ray.

Patty, still standing close to Snow, said, "Remember, we do not know who called for Badeel's number. Beside from that worry, you have had us all worried lately. You have been working long hours and then it was a shock to you when you saw Joy."

"You may be right, Mom."

Jack added, "Snow, I truly believe that the smartest thing is for you and your mother to leave as soon as possible. Make your arrangements and then hit the road."

Patty looked at Snow, smiling widely, and said, "We're going on a road trip, yeah!"

"Mom, you always find the best way to look at things."

"Hopefully, with the help of Homeland Security, we will have Ali and his brother locked up before you get back home."

Ray moved toward Patty and Snow. "I hope your grandpa is right. We have been under a large amount of stress because of these two creeps."

"Omar, will you and your mother meet with me and our family attorney in the morning at 10 am?"

"Yes, Jack, we will be there."

"I want our attorney on this. He probably will have some ideas on how to get your wife Irma here as soon as possible. I think if we can inform the right people about the current situation, they will understand that Irma is in extreme danger in that country."

Chapter Twenty-Three

Road Trip

Ray thought that Jack was right, and so he called the four hotels that he knew he would be staying at and reserved two two-bedroom suites at each. Ray had a plan, and he had put together an itinerary he was proud of. He allowed plenty of time for travel and to visit some of the sites in the towns along the way. He knew how excited Patty was about the road trip. He decided that he would give her one she would never forget.

The first stop on the road trip was in Atlanta. After the trio checked into the Ritz, Ray made no haste in finding his way to the Aquarium. The Georgia Aquarium is amazing, Patty told him. They were delighted to see the sharks and watch the dolphins play. Ray then surprised them with a visit to CNN Studios, which Ray found very fascinating. The girls were excited because Ray had promised a tour over Atlanta in a helicopter. "Mom, this is breathtaking, so beautiful. The buildings looked as if they are adorned in jewels."

"I love it," said Patty as she smiled and gazed out of the window.

❖ ❖ ❖ ❖ ❖

They were tired and ready to sleep when they arrived late back at the Ritz of Atlanta.

The next morning, Ray woke the girls up with a question, "Are you ready to visit the amazing Rock City on top of Lookout mountain?"

"Yes," Snow shouted. She was so excited, she rushed into the shower. Unpacking her bags, she noticed a man's shaving kit. "How did Ray's shaving kit get into my luggage? Must have been a mix up when the Doorman brought the luggage up," she thought to herself.

* * * * *

After everyone had their showers and ate a hearty breakfast, they were again on their way. The trip to Chattanooga was filled with talk and laughter. They stood on top of Lookout Mountain, looking down at the quilt-like patch work that made up the diverse life styles and communities. "This is the country I love, we are just like this. We are people from all over the world, knitted together to make a great nation," said Patty.

"Mom, looking down from this mountain gives me a new perspective on life, our problems seem insignificant when I look at the grand design," said Snow.

Patty agreed and said, "I'm overwhelmed with this amazing view, the trail, and the caverns here at Lookout Mountain." The trio then cruised on the Pride of the South. They all enjoyed the delicious dinner and sightseeing along the river on what Ray called "a totally relaxing cruise."

* * * * *

Ray was excited when they neared Chicago. They headed for the Shedd Aquarium, then went on to the Sears Tower Skydeck and then spending the remaining of the afternoon at the Field Museum. They excitedly rode the guided Bus to the Underworld where they were able to see the sites of some of the Chicago mob crimes, and they heard stories about John Dillinger and Hymie Weiss. They checked in at the Ritz of Chicago in the early morning hours. Next stop after a good night sleep was the Gateway Arch.

The tired road trip threesome arrived in St. Louis and check in at the Ritz Carlton. Patty and Ray made love despite being tired. Snow passed out as soon as her head hit the pillow but was alarmed when she woke up sitting, looking out of the balcony of her room. Snow stood up confused. She walked into the bathroom to start her shower. As she reached for the faucet, she saw the shaving kit again. She couldn't help herself from opening it up. There was a black Kinowear shirt that would bulk up any wearer into a muscular profile. There was also a red mustache, a red wig, and sun glasses. What kind of kinky thing is Ray and Mom doing? she thought to herself.

The last stop of the honeymoon was spent in Kansas City, Missouri. They stopped at the Stadiums along Interstate 70 as they were arriving into the city. They stayed at the Intercontinental at the Plaza. They enjoyed a reasonable dinner at Gates Barbecue and then went to the House of Blues for some entertainment. They went back to the hotel early because Snow complained of a dreadful headache. Patty and Ray were delighted to return to the hotel early.

* * * * *

Back in Iran, Irma received a call from Ali, "Hello, Irma, Badeel told me that Joy and Omar went to the U.S. You know he will bring them home. You need to leave your mother's house and come home, so we can all live in peace. You and Omar are very blessed by Allah and should continue to show the obedience to the law."

"Yes, I know this," Irma replied, "we have been blessed."

"Irma, Badeel had wanted me to go with him. His plan is also to bring Snow home. He believes that Snow belongs to him. I tried to convince him to leave Snow in America, I know she belongs there. She has a man she wants to marry. I saw them together, and she looked happy with him. But Badeel will not listen to me."

"That is true, Badeel will listen to no one," she agreed.

"Irma, if you return home, I will not let Badeel hurt you. I have guilt because I was not able to protect my mother, and the day she died, I swore to her I would not let anyone ever get hurt like she did."

"Ali, you can't keep me safe!"

"Yes, I will, I will defend you. Irma, I was wrong when I was young. I thought if I took a captive wife, she would never leave me, and I could do whatever I wanted to her. But I became her captive because I loved her. I think often about what I did and why. Part of me did it so no one could stone her for wanting a divorce. I know it sounds crazy, and really, I was crazy then. You know my daughter Snow helps people. I think Badeel should leave her there. She can help people that are mentally sick. But he won't listen, and she will need someone to help her live here. Please, come back."

"Ali, you wouldn't be able to protect her either. I hope Badeel cannot find her and she can live in America and be happy."

"Irma, Badeel will find her, he knows where she is. If you come back, you can help her adjust. You both are young women. Think about it and come home. He said he will be back in two days."

"I will think about what you said. Good bye, Ali."

● ● ● ● ●

When Irma hung up the phone with Ali, she immediately called Omar. "Omar, we have to act now. Badeel is in America."

"Wait by the phone, I will speak with Jack now." Omar called Jack, and Jack called his contacts. The decision was made to help her get out of Iran while Badeel could not interfere. And within 24 hours, Omar and Irma were reunited in the states.

Jack skyped his brother and friends, informing them that Badeel was in the country. Homeland security was notified, and Jack called Ray to update him on the current situation with Irma and to alert him that Badeel was in the states.

Badeel was in the states, and actually at that time, he was checking into his room at the Elms in Excelsior Springs. He had two bodyguards with him and his Beretta Mx4 Storm. Why would anyone want to come here for a honeymoon? he thought. But this was precisely the place that his American contact had told him to come and to check in. He was eagerly awaiting the next phone call. He knew it would only be days until he would be able to avenge himself against Martha, the wicked American Woman. He thought to himself that soon he would be taking Snow back to her rightful home in Iran. She belonged to him, and as a woman, she would spend the rest of her days submitting to him. Badeel laughed out loud, his thoughts made him joyous, and he was at peace knowing he would successfully complete his plans and that his guards stood watch in the room next to him.

His phone rang, it was his contact from the states. The voice on the other end told him, "Yes, they will be checking in tomorrow. They are coming there because they wanted to use the mineral springs on the grounds. Yes, Snow is with them and precautions are needed and must be taken since the authorities have been alerted. Yes, we will meet you tonight. Remember, I will be expecting the $100,000 when we meet,"

The Elms had dim lights and were in its relaxed state. People were unwinding for the night. Badeel decided to take a walk around the grounds. His guards concealed themselves within the shadows. Badeel found it interesting to be housed at the famous Elms. He noticed the stone surrounding the grounds was the same stone they used in building the massive Elms hotel.

Miles away from the Elms was a lone rider on the road that night. He was focused on reaching his destination and following through with his own plans. "First, to the clubhouse, so I can meet up with the brothers, and then on to the Elms," he said to himself.

• • • • •

There was a knock on the clubhouse door. The dogs began to bark and Lunatic, the enforcer, came to the door. "Frank, Dude is here," he turned and said to the brothers inside.

"Yeah, settle the dogs down and bring him in," Lunatic used hand signs, and the dogs quickly sat down and did not even whimper.

Dude walked in through the hallway, noticing the large aquariums that were installed in the walls. He looked closely into one and saw that rattle snakes were the inhabitants and the inhibitors. Dude heard Frank yell at him from another room, "Are you ready to ride, brother?" Dude followed Lunatic into the meeting room. Frank gave Dude a big hug, slapping him on the back with both hands. "Lunatic, Cisco, and Ted are riding with us," Frank said.

"Great!" snorted Dude, "but how about a beer. I have been travelling here for hours."

"Of course, hey, Cisco, how about grabbing a couple brews for us. Here is a couple bucks for the kitty, I'm buying Dude's," Frank said.

After a couple beers and some small talk, the four men grabbed their jackets, and Frank told them they were not to wear their colors for this trip. Frank said, "I think we will need our chaps tonight, it's still a bit nippy. Meet you out by the garage."

Dude went out front to his bike. Lunatic followed him out and then went back into a bedroom and grabbed a pillow case. He then stopped off at the aquariums. He used his snake stick to snag out four of the snakes. He placed them one by one into the pillow case and then put them in a snake container that fit his saddle bags.

The group was waiting for him outside. The men stood each one next to their bikes, tightening up bandanas, gloves, and other riding gear. After Lunatic came out and rolled his bike out, he went back and secured the door. Then he hit a button on his transponder that opened up the security gate.

Frank yelled out, "Let's ride!" Each man mounted his bike. It seemed as if they all started their bikes up in unison. Dude could hear the roar of the other four Harley engines, then started his own bike, he fell into the pack as they rode out into the chilly night. Lunatic hit his transponder again, and the security gate closed. As they took off towards the highway, the sounds of the engines rumbled, breaking through the silence of the night. The only warmth was coming up from the engines.

The ride was cold, the streets were clear of snow, but snow still gleamed from off the grass. They soon approached the driveway that curved going up to the tall stone building with an American flag flying proudly above. The group rode up to the front of the Elms. They parked their bikes on the side of the drive and dismounted. "Dude, do you have the room number?" asked Frank.

"Yeah, it's 325."

"One of Cisco's girls is working tonight. Let's wait out here until he finds out what's up."

Cisco walked up and into the lobby. There she was, his sweet and petite Chandra working at the desk. Cisco looked around and saw an empty lobby. He looked at her, and she looked up toward the security camera and motioned him to follow her behind a partition. Once safely behind, they embraced, exchanging kisses.

"So, are you going to give me a room key for later tonight? What time are you getting off?"

"I'll be off at 4 am," she said as she handed him a room key.

"What did you find out about that guy from Iran?" he asked her.

"Well, he looks awfully mean, and he came in with two other big guys. They each had a case with them. The rich looking one had a small case, too. The mean looking rich guy is in his own suite, the other two are sharing a room. He booked room 325, and they are both in 311."

"Okay, Chandra, you're the best. See you later, and oh, text me if you see anything unusual."

Cisco went back outside to his friends and said, "Okay, I got a key. Let's go in on the side. Chandra said there are two other guys in 311. She will text me if she spots anything."

The men went in the side entry and walked quietly up the three flights of stairs. Once in the hallway, they walked toward the door marked 325. Dude knocked on the door. Badeel looked through the peep hole, then opened the door. Three of the men walked in with Dude, Lunatic leaned back and stood next to the door, so Badeel would not see that he was the fourth man. Once in the room, Dude looked around, observing his surroundings.

"Well, Badeel, I'm glad to welcome you back to our country. Before tonight is over, you will have your revenge and your woman."

"Good, now get right to the business at hand here. Have they arrived yet?" asked Badeel.

"No, they are not expected to arrive until 5 am. We want to bring you up to date on our plan, but first, let me introduce you to three of the most hated men in America. This is Frank, Cisco, and Ted." The three men just stared at him as Dude said their names.

"Why are these men hated so much, what have they done?"

Dude laughed, "Well, first, they are males, then they are white, and then they ride Harley Davidsons!"

"I don't understand," said Badeel.

"It's a cultural thing, guess you wouldn't get it. But I tell you, these men would die for an innocent!"

"Business, business, I do not have time for riddles," Badeel said in a rough voice, "please explain the plan."

"We are waiting for our coordinator, the guy who hired us and put this all together. He will be here soon. In the meantime, we thought you might want to toast to the success of our mission."

"No, I do not drink," Badeel proudly stated.

"What the hell!" yelled Frank. "I cannot trust a man that will not drink with us. Let's go."

"Just wait a moment. We will be missing out on our take. Plus, I have expenses," argued Dude.

"So what, we are out of here," voiced Frank as he headed toward the door.

"Badeel, what's one drink?" urged Dude.

"Huh?" said Badeel.

"I need to show my guys that you are righteous!" pleaded Dude.

Badeel, realizing that his chance for revenge and to get Snow was about to walk out the door, said, "Okay, I agree to have one drink with you, my new friends."

Frank brought out his flask. Smiling, he walked around the room grabbing five glasses. This is all American, 100% moonshine. Putting a healthy pour in the five glasses, he handed each man one. "Bottoms up." The men clicked their glasses and then Badeel followed suit, taking a deep gulp. Badeel started gagging as the other men laughed.

As soon as Badeel had finished his drink, Frank punched in Lunatic's number on his phone. Lunatic felt his phone vibrate and looked at the screen. He quietly and promptly walked to room 311. Using a card reader, he ran it in the door. As soon as the green light flashed, Lunatic opened the door and bent down, shaking the pillow case out, letting the vipers out into the room. "Strike as you will," he whispered. Then leaning against the hotel wall, he folded his arms to wait.

Lunatic stood next to door of 311 for only 15 minutes before one man came running out, where he met face-to-face with Lunatic. The man was able to just catch a glimpse of Lunatic's balled up fist that was coming straight toward his face. The punch hit him square in the jaw and he fell backwards, hitting the floor. Lunatic carefully peered into the room. He saw a man lying still on the tile floor. He pulled out his snake stick and deliberately gave his wrist a flick extending the stick. He then carefully walked in the room, taking the pillow case out from the inside of his vest pocket. He stepped over the body and gathered up his brew of vipers. Once back in the hallway, he put them back into their carry case.

"Well done, now it's time to go back to the clubhouse. You will be dining on your favorite spread, got you some frogs, lizards, and a big old rat." He then threw the sheet over the man lying in the hallway. He bent down, picking the man up effortlessly and throwing him over his back. Then Lunatic walked out to his bike. He threw the man on the backseat of his bike. He rapped a bungee cord around him, then secured it to the back rest. He then placed a piece of duct tape over his mouth and then taped his hands together behind him, as well as securing his feet to the pegs. He had future plans for his passenger. Lunatic then straddled his bike and rode off back towards the clubhouse.

Chapter Twenty-Four

The Welcome

Badeel, feeling the effects from the moonshine, was having a hard time using his phone.

Dude asked him, "Is everything all right?"

Badeel just sneered at his phone.

Dude, looking down at his phone, said, "Okay, I'm leaving, and I will return with the man."

Badeel was fumbling with his phone as Dude closed the door. Once the door was closed, Frank turned to Badeel and hit him in the head with the butt of his 45 cal. Then he quickly threw Badeel on the floor, duct taping his hands and feet together. He then lifted Badeel up and positioned him in a dinette chair. Frank poured another round, "Bottoms up!" he said. Then he poured a drink down Badeel's throat. Badeel began coughing and choking. As Badeel gasped for air, he asked, "What are you doing?"

The men in the room heard a soft knock on door 325, Frank looked out. "Pizza time, delivery," someone said on the other side of the door.

Frank then opened the door, and Bud stepped through with a pizza. "Let's eat some pizza! Badeel, I'll bet you do not have anything like the Elms back in Iran. Don't you think that the stone work is impressive?

Frank, they do not have anything like this pizza there either. Would you like a slice, Badeel?"

"No, I do not eat that stuff!"

Frank turned around and speedily injected Badeel, his eyes flew open, both angry and shocked. "It's been a pleasure, Mr. Badeel, to let you sample some of our homemade moonshine, and I hope you enjoyed the lift from the cocaine, too."

"Hello, Badeel. It's been a long time since I saw your ugly face."

"Who are you, I don't know who you are?"

"Are you sure," Bud said, taking off his sunglasses, looking directly into Badeel's eyes.

"You look somewhat familiar but no, who are you?"

"Well, I know you, and Frank here knows all about you," Bud said, confidently smiling at him.

"What are you talking about?"

"Well, it was quite a few years back, when Frank first heard the name Badeel. I was almost 16, and I was treating myself to, what you might call, a coming of age bash. I had just left a group of people I was infused with. I left with hope and excitement. Thought I might come out this way to the Springs, hoping the minerals might heal me of my ADHD."

"I do not understand you," groaned out Badeel.

"Anyway, no matter, you will. I came here to the Springs, I found a man, shot, laying in the road, so I helped him. I asked him what he needed, and he handed me a card with his name and address on it. So, I drove him there. It was a biker's clubhouse here in the Springs. Once I was able to explain and get through the security, I found out that he was the President of the chapter. He told me he was shot off of his bike by a rival club, they thought he was dead when they saw he was hit and how he went down. He said he played dead as they took his bike. He said I was there just in time at the right moment. He said I saved his life and that he knew they would send their enforcer back within minutes to make sure that he was dead. Am I telling it right so far, Frank?"

"Sounds about right to me."

Bud continued. "This man was grateful and so were his brothers. He asked if there was anything he could do for me. That's when I told him about you, I told him about a man that came from Iran, that had raped a nine-year-old girl named Snow. I told them this man justified his savage act by saying that she was his wife. And that this man named Badeel had planned on taking her forcibly to Iran to live. After that night, I just waited. Knowing that Frank was an honorable man, I knew he would come through for me someday. I haven't been in contact with Frank until about a month ago. That's when I pulled out his card, the card he had given me so long ago. I called his number on the card, and to my amazement, he answered. I told him that the evil man was coming back to America. I told him that he would have some friends with him. By the way, where is your brother, Ali, we had expected one more?"

Badeel, speaking with a slur, said, "He refused to come."

"We will talk about that later. Now, I will continue. Frank asked what I needed him to do. Not much, just for him to plan a trip to the Elms to meet you. So, here we all are. Thanks, Frank!"

Frank nodded and asked, "Is there anything else you need?"

Badeel interjected, "This is a mistake, I was told to come here."

Bud pulled out a rope from his back pack. "I would be holding to you if you stand him up on that chair, take this rope, and tie it to the light fixture up there, then make a noose out of the other end and put it around his neck."

Frank did as Bud asked him.

"Frank, by the way, where are his two friends?"

"I believe Lunatic was entertaining them with his rattle snake collection. No one has ever walked away happy from an encounter with Lunatic's vipers. Matter of fact, they don't walk away at all!"

"Thank you, Frank. I can take it from here."

"Okay, Buddy, if you ever need anything, just give me a call, you've got my card."

"Thanks for helping to right this wrong."

"Don't sweat it, and we will do the cleanup in room 311. Don't worry, I got it, Buddy."

Frank and Ted left and calmly walked towards room 311. They cleaned up after Lunatic and took the dead body with them. Cisco went to his room, where he sat patiently playing a game on his phone, waiting for Chandra to end her shift.

"Badeel, we are alone now. I hope you don't mind if I video this little interaction that is going to take place here on my phone. Dude should be back anytime. Where is that money? I want to get it out for him. He gets 50 and I get 50. "

"I'm not going to tell you that," he mumbled defiantly.

"Have it your way. No need to let Dude interrupt us." Bud started to move the chair from underneath Badeel.

Badeel quickly changed his mind about talking. "It's in the box in the first drawer of the dresser. It's nothing to me anyway, it's just pocket change."

"I thank you, Badeel, for your pocket change. I will be able to use it, so Snow can start a new life."

Bud opened the dresser and pulled out the box. There was a large, black, leather wallet and in the wallet was $100,000 in hundred-dollar bills.

"Thank you for the payment, Badeel, so nice of you. But as the mother always said, the show must go on. I'm going to start this video now. Are you at all curious? Do you wonder who I'm going to show this video to?"

"What! No, I don't care about your stupid video! I demand you to cut me lose and to let me go!"

"Let you go? I promise I'm going to let you go. But first and foremost, I'm making this video for Snow. I want her to see the villain she still has nightmares about. The brutal rape you inflicted on her small body." Turning away, Bud started to record. "Hello, Snow, this is Bud, I never left you, nor will I ever leave, we need each other."

"Badeel, where is Ali, and why isn't he here?" Bud asked.

Badeel refused to talk until Bud put his foot on the chair again.

Badeel then disclosed rapidly, "Ali doesn't want to ever come back to your evil rotten country. He said he came back to see Martha and that she was happy and so was his daughter Snow. He said the only gift he could give them was staying away. Martha took what was mine, and he refused to help me. I will someday get my revenge on Martha for turning my brother's heart against me and keeping me from my wife."

"What wife, Badeel?"

"Snow!" Badeel shouted. "I was lied to, I was told that Snow would be here."

"She was never your wife, she was your victim! But after she sees this video, she will be free from you." Looking at the video phone, Bud said, "Snow, this is why I'm doing all of this, for you, for your empowerment. I also have to tell you, I hired Dude. He is a Private Detective. He might hunt you down. If so, just leave me a voicemail or letter, I'll take care of it. Also, he is getting half of the money. I'm depositing the rest in our account. Oh, one more thing before the show starts, I know you have went through a lot of school, and you have worked very hard for your licensure. But, you might want to rethink being a therapist, you might also want to rethink Duane. He is too boring for us. Now, I can see you with a man like Dude. And you will make a much better detective than therapist. Okay, the show must go on. Bud presents, 'Letting Badeel Go.'"

Bud then turned toward Badeel. "Badeel, in your own country, the family of the victim carries out the sentence of the guilty party. Badeel, you are found guilty of the rape of Snow DuTro and in aiding and abetting your brother Ali in the kidnapping and imprisonment of Martha DuTro, Snow's mother. For those crimes, you are to be set free. I have learned this lesson from you, it is double talk. It's twisting the truth, so much so, it looks something like the truth, but it is a sinister lie."

"Let me go now, I demand it, people will be knocking down that door at any moment coming for me, you do not know who I am!" he said, trying to intimidate and scare Bud.

Bud declared in a loud voice, "Badeel, I do know who you are. I will set you free. I now set you free from your own evilness and cruel acts. I'm Snow's closest friend, and I take revenge for her!" Bud then kicked the chair out from underneath Badeel. Bud watched as Badeel hung there, twisting and gasping for air until all the life that was in Badeel was gone. Snow, don't worry! I know how to clean a room. Good night, sweet girl, good night!"

Bud cleaned and wiped down the room. He took his cash and left Dude's for him. He took off his plastic gloves after closing the door from the outside of the room.

Moments later after Bud left, Dude knocked on the door, finding it unlocked, he pushed it open. As he slowly pushed the door open, he called out, "Hello, anybody here? Couldn't find Bud." As he cautiously glanced around the room, he saw Badeel hanging from the rope that was attached to the light fixture. He saw the chair lying on the floor. He knew Badeel was dead. He then saw the cash on the table. What happened here, he thought. Definitely not good for this guy! He could already visualize the night news headlines, "Iranian terrorist found dead hanging in a hotel room at the famous Elms hotel." He quickly grabbed the money, wiped down the room, and then closed the door from the outside. He ran back down the stairs, mounted his bike, and rode off.

There was still one bike left standing alone on the side of the building. At 4:30 am, Cisco left his love hookup and walked back down the stairs to room 325. After walking into the room and observing the scene, he walked over to the bed and took a sheet off. He then picked up the chair, laid the sheet on the floor, eased the body of Badeel down, dropping it on the sheets. He wrapped the sheet around the body, tied it up with the rope, and wiped the room down. He hoisted Badeel over his shoulders and then closed the door from the outside. Once outside,

Cisco walked across the grounds. He walked far into the back of the Elms. He walked until he reached the excavating pit. He stopped over to the edge and kicked a rock down. He watched as it rolled and hit the side, loosening more rocks as it fell. He then dropped Badeel off the edge. He then kicked more of the rocks off from the side. He had to jump back as the rock slide began. Soon, all of the falling rocks buried Badeel's body deep under the rock pile. Cisco kicked and jumped on more rocks, creating another landslide. When he was satisfied that he had sufficiently buried Badeel underneath layers of stone, he turned away, went back to his bike, and rode away into the night back toward the clubhouse, thinking only of his and Chandra's love making.

Snow woke up the following morning again, sitting on the balcony. This time she noticed she had a phone in her hand. She also had a note in her other hand. It said, "Play the video." She brought her hand to her mouth as she gasped, that's when she felt it, something above her lip? It was a fake mustache glued above her lip!

After the honeymoon trip, Jack received a phone call from a detective in Kansas City. The man on the phone spoke in a deep, low voice, "Jack, I was told to call you. Please do not ask any questions, just listen. You, nor any of your family members, will ever be threatened again by Badeel". Then the phone went dead. Jack called an emergency family meeting to inform the family circle of the phone call. They all agreed never to share that information with anyone, and to carry on as if Badeel had never darkened their lives.

Chapter Twenty-Five

Conclusion

The next Valentine's Day was the best ever for Patty and Ray. Even though they still hadn't gone on their real honeymoon, Hotel SANE had continued to grow in popularity. Patty was back as the opening act. Her and Ray were more in love than ever. Ray and Duane had opened a new outreach program at the community center where more of the population could be served.

Jack and Anna went to Ireland and were engaging the beautiful country side with each other on a well-deserved vacation. Jack finally felt as if his family was safe and that he and Anna could enjoy their retirement.

Joy, Omar, and his wife Irma bought a beautiful home on the beach close to hotel SANE. Omar had inherited a substantial amount of his father's wealth due to the fact that his father had disappeared. He would be the sole beneficiary of his father's estate in six years.

Snow resigned from the Community Center, and she called off her wedding. She explained to Duane why she couldn't marry him and broke off their engagement. Duane promised to keep her secret.

Snow interviewed for a job on the police force and was hired and is working toward becoming a detective. She is dating a man from Kansas

City, Missouri and had adjusted back to the Midwest and the fields full of amber waves of grains.

Ali had another regret, that he did not stop his brother from going to America. Ali sat alone, hoping that Badeel would contact him or that someone might come forth with information about his brother's whereabouts. He hoped he was still alive but felt that he was not, after all, it had been almost a year since he had last heard from him. If only he knew what had happened to his brother, he could move on.

And me, I am working undercover with Dude. Dude was able to meet with Dr. Rose, and he presented our proposal where we would lease the Dome for ten years from the hospital. With Dr. Rose's influence, I now have a very peaceful, obscure place to live and conduct my business. I plan on informing Snow, but time is on my side. You understand, I know all of Snow's thoughts, desires, and ideas. Snow, she knows only what I tell her. She is on a need to know basis. Don't worry about me, I have a good plan. As long as I stay on my Adderall, I'll be fine. You see, I understand that it's not our disabilities that define us but it's our abilities. Our limitations should not stifle us, but our creativity should stir our minds beyond natural limits, kind of like pizza!

SNOW AT THE DOME

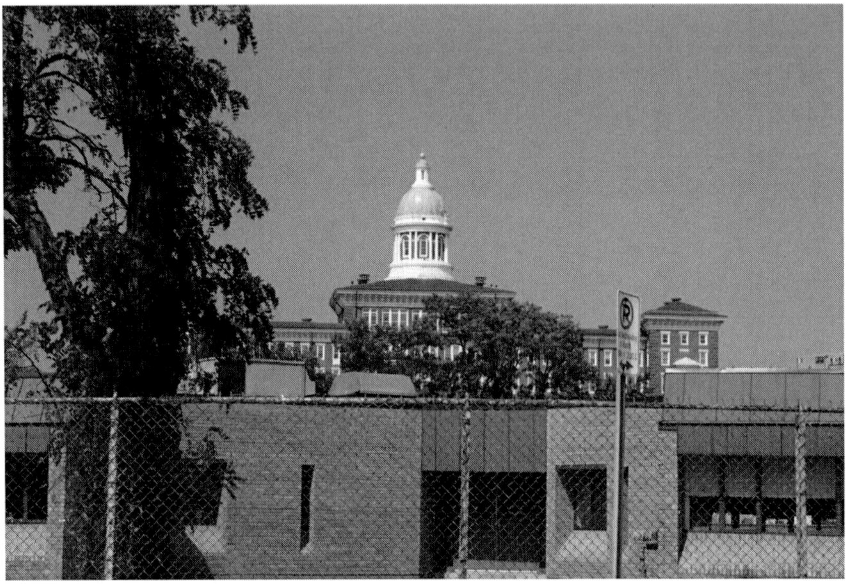